altar-ed ❀
❀ plans

altar-ed  plans

REBECCA CORNISH TALLEY

Bonneville
Springville, Utah

The views expressed within this work are the sole responsibility of the author and do not necessarily reflect the position of Cedar Fort, Inc., or any other entity.

This is a work of fiction. The characters, names, incidents, places, and dialogue are products of the author's imagination, and are not to be construed as real.

ISBN 13: 978-1-59955-280-4

Published by Bonneville, an imprint of Cedar Fort, Inc., 2373 W. 700 S., Springville, UT 84663. Distributed by Cedar Fort, Inc., www.cedarfort.com

LIBRARY OF CONGRESS CATALOGING-IN-PUBLICATION DATA

Library of Congress Cataloging-in-Publication Data

Talley, Rebecca Cornish.
  Altar-ed Plans / Rebecca Cornish Talley.
    p. cm.
  ISBN 978-1-59955-280-4 (acid-free paper)
  1. Brides--Fiction. 2. Man-woman relationships--Fiction. 3. Mormon women--Fiction. I. Title.
  PS3620.A5374W56 2009
  813'.6--dc22
                                        2009008912

Cover design by Jen Boss
Cover design © 2009 by Lyle Mortimer
Edited and typeset by Melissa J. Caldwell

Printed in the United States of America

10 9 8 7 6 5 4 3 2 1

Printed on acid-free paper

Dedication

To my friends at LDStorymakers, Authors Incognito, and
ANWA, who understand the dream and support me in mine.

To Terry Montague for answering endless questions
and pushing me to improve my writing skills.

To my grandmother, Norma, for her words
of encouragement through the years.

To my sister, Ashlie, and her family for their love
and enthusiastic support.

To all of my creative children, who constantly amaze me with
their talents, and who encourage me to reach
for the stars in developing mine.

Most of all, to my husband, who inspired this story,
who is my best cheerleader, and who will always
be my one true, eternal love.

one

Her wedding day. A day she'd never forget. A perfect day that would begin her perfect life with her perfect husband. It couldn't be anything but perfect because that's how she'd planned it.

Caitlyn grabbed her hand mirror. She tucked a wisp of her dark blond hair behind her ear as she examined her makeup for the hundredth time. The hum of the engine was the only sound in the car.

"You look beautiful," her mom said as she turned from the front seat of the car to look at Caitlyn. "The temple isn't too far away; are you getting nervous?"

"Kind of. But, I don't know why. After all, I've been planning this day for so long and everything is falling into place." A smile spread across her face, lighting up her eyes. "By this afternoon, I'll be Caitlyn Haggerty." She couldn't help but feel the joy as it bubbled to the surface. Soon Justin would be her husband, and she wanted nothing more than to spend her life, and all of eternity, loving him.

"I'm glad it all worked out for you," her younger sister said with a shrug.

Caitlyn jerked her head back and gave Lindsay an incredulous look. "Did you think it wouldn't?"

"I figured you'd meet another guy while you were at BYU. I

didn't think you'd actually wait for him." Lindsay snatched a tube of lip gloss from Caitlyn's makeup bag.

"Seriously?"

Lindsay shrugged again.

"No way. Justin is the only one for me. Has been since high school. I can't imagine my life without him." She paused. "And, after today, I won't have to. We'll be married and all my dreams will come true." A vision of Justin's smiling face with his sky-blue eyes and blond, wavy hair flashed across her mind.

"So," Lindsay said as she applied the lip gloss, "where's he been for the last few days?"

"Huh?" Caitlyn blinked her eyes a few times.

"He didn't even come over for Christmas dinner."

"Your point?"

"Shouldn't your fiancé have eaten Christmas dinner with you?"

"He wanted to spend time with his family. He's sweet like that. And then he went down to Newport Beach to see an old companion. You know, bachelor stuff."

"Isn't that kind of weird?"

"No. Not at all. We'll have plenty of Christmases together. I think it's fine he wanted to spend time with his family and with Troy." It was fine. Just because they didn't spend Christmas together like she'd hoped didn't mean anything. They'd be sealed today and have the rest of their lives and eternity to be together. It wasn't weird. Caitlyn assured herself that Lindsay was still a teenager and didn't understand such things.

"Whatever you say. I—"

"Let's not talk about it anymore. It's my wedding day, and I only want happy thoughts." She gazed at herself in the mirror and recalled their first date when Justin had tried to teach her to surf. She kept falling off the board into the cool ocean water, sometimes even slipping below the surface. She could almost taste the salt on her lips.

When he placed his arms around her to help steady her on the board, her skin tingled, and it wasn't because she was cold.

She closed her eyes and immersed herself in memories of Justin's embrace.

"Cait . . . Cait . . . Cait?" Lindsay intruded on her daydream.

"Huh?"

"Mom asked if you double-checked everything before we left the house."

Caitlyn did a mental tally of the contents of the trunk. "The garment bag with my dress and veil. My shoes—"

"You're sure," her mother asked.

"Yes. The photographer will be in the courtyard so he can capture us as soon as we come out of the temple, right?"

"That's what he said when I called yesterday," her mother answered.

"I think everything is all in place then," Caitlyn said, happiness enveloping her.

"As long as Justin shows up." Lindsay let out a laugh.

Caitlyn gave her a look. "Ha. Ha."

"I still don't agree with the rules about your Mormon temples. A father should be able to see his daughter's wedding," her dad said over his shoulder, his voice stern.

"Dad, we've already discussed this a thousand times."

"I don't understand why the Episcopal Church where your mom and I were married wasn't an option. All Saints by the Sea is a beautiful building right near the ocean, and all of our family could've attended."

"Because I want to be sealed for eternity. I don't want to marry Justin for this life—"

"Caitlyn—"

"Robert," her mom interrupted. She squeezed his arm, "Please, not today. Cait's made her decision, and this is her day. Let's not ruin it with another argument."

"You'll be able to see the ceremony," her father said to her mother. "It isn't right. A church shouldn't separate families on a day like today."

A few moments of silence followed. Her dad finally said, "I'm sorry, Caitie. You know how much I love you. I'm disappointed, that's all. I've looked forward to your wedding day ever since I first held you in my arms."

Caitlyn reached up and patted her dad's shoulder. "I know, but this is the right thing for me to do. I'll see you as soon as we come out. You'll be the first one I hug."

"Looks like the weather will cooperate," her mom offered. Caitlyn recognized it as her mom's usual attempt at peacemaking.

Caitlyn gazed out of the window of her parents' silver Jaguar. "I sure miss California weather. I can't wait until Justin and I both graduate and we can move back to Santa Barbara and start our family. We'll have two boys and two girls."

"Sounds like you have it all planned out," her mom said. She laughed.

"What?"

"Not everything goes as planned, you know. You may end up with all boys or all girls."

"Four children? Do you have any idea how expensive it is to raise kids these days? Especially in Santa Barbara. You need to be realistic," her dad said.

"Don't worry. I have it all figured out. Justin thinks I'm obsessed with planning everything, but that's his way of saying he appreciates me taking charge." Caitlyn nodded her head.

"Where will you work?" her father asked.

"Me? I'm not going to work. I plan to stay home and raise the kids."

"You can't be serious."

"I want to be at home and take care of our house and the kids while Justin works and eventually takes over his dad's business."

"You're going to waste your education raising kids?" her dad asked.

Her mom cut in, "We'll be at the temple in less than fifteen minutes. Robert, you charged the video camera and brought extra batteries for the digital camera, correct?"

"The batteries are in the camera bag."

"I want to make sure we get plenty of footage. Maybe you can record them while Lindsay takes photos."

"What about the photographer?" her dad asked.

"He'll get plenty of shots, but I want my own, especially of the family and everyone who will be waiting outside the temple."

Caitlyn's parents continued to discuss taking pictures. She was grateful that her mom had sidetracked her dad. She laid her head back against the seat and shut her eyes. In a few hours, she'd start eternity with the guy she'd loved since high school.

"I can see the temple," Lindsay said.

Caitlyn bent down so she could view the temple from Lindsay's window. "I've always thought it looked a little out of place. I mean, L.A. is city everywhere, and all you can see is pavement and then, boom, the temple sitting on that big grassy hill. It looks so heavenly."

She smoothed her hair again and took several breaths to calm her nerves as she gazed at the white building set against the clear blue sky. This was it.

They pulled into the parking lot, and Caitlyn's heart felt like it might jump out of her throat. Since the temple was only open this one day during Christmas break, she had to go through the endowment session right before her wedding ceremony. She worried it might be too overwhelming, but it was the only option if they wanted to be married before winter semester at BYU.

Caitlyn walked around to the back of the car and opened the trunk. She rummaged through the contents. "Mom, I can't find my veil."

Her mom stepped over to the car. "I thought you said everything was in there."

"I put it in here. I'm sure of it. Where did it go?"

"Could it be in with your dress?"

Caitlyn unzipped the garment bag and searched through it. "I don't see it." Her face heated. Stress clamped down on her chest. "I can't have pictures without my veil."

"Calm down. We'll figure it out."

"How can it not be here? This will ruin my wedding!"

"Cait, you're being way too dramatic. Get a hold of yourself. We'll work something out, and it will be fine."

"Mom, this is my one and only wedding day. I wanted it to be perfect, and now my veil is missing."

Her mother checked her watch. "We need to get inside the temple. Your endowment session will begin in less than an hour and you need to prepare. You don't need your veil until you leave the temple after the ceremony. I'll make some calls and see if someone can go to the house and find it and then bring it down here." She cupped Caitlyn's chin in her hand. "Your day will be perfect, and you will be a beautiful bride."

Caitlyn closed her eyes and contained her breathing. She opened her eyes and said, "Thanks, Mom. And thanks for coming with me. I know it's hard for you to go to the temple without Dad, but I'm so happy you'll be with me."

"Me too. I wouldn't miss my baby getting married for anything." Her mom wiped at her eyes.

"Mom, don't get me started. I'm emotional enough."

Caitlyn and her mother embraced.

Lindsay approached them. "I'll take Dad over to the visitor's center. Maybe he'll like it. Or not."

Caitlyn and her mother walked to the entrance of the temple and opened the large door. Caitlyn noticed the sign that said, "Members Only," and wished her Dad could accompany them. She stepped inside, toward the desk.

She and her mom waited behind another couple and their parents, while a different couple stood in the waiting area holding garment bags. It was a busy day for the temple. She held her bag tightly. "I wonder if Justin is here yet. I can't wait to see him."

"I assume they're here." Her mom reached over and adjusted Caitlyn's necklace.

After a few minutes, the outside door opened, and Caitlyn turned to see Justin's parents. She grinned.

Justin's father motioned for her to come out to him. She looked at her mom, and they both exited the temple.

"Hello, Caitlyn," he said in a strained voice. He seemed distracted. Caitlyn figured it was due to the impending events of the day.

"Hi." She craned her neck to see if she could catch a glimpse of her way hot, soon-to-be groom. Excitement welled up inside.

"I . . . we . . . well . . ." Justin's dad stammered.

"Where's Justin?" Caitlyn said with a smile.

Justin's mom stepped forward. Her eyes were bloodshot. "We have some . . . bad news."

Suddenly, Caitlyn couldn't breathe. She felt like someone was gripping her neck so tight she couldn't swallow. She eked out, "Is something wrong?"

The Haggertys both nodded.

Caitlyn clapped her hand to her mouth. Terrifying thoughts swirled in her mind. "What is it?"

Brother Haggerty began, "You know Justin came down here to spend time with Troy."

Caitlyn nodded. Tears formed in her eyes while her imagination exploded.

"He . . . well . . ."

"Is he okay?" Caitlyn's voice cracked.

"In a manner of speaking," his mother said. She shook her head.

"Please, tell us what's wrong," Caitlyn's mother said.

"We were supposed to meet for breakfast early this morning." His dad kicked at the ground. "Justin didn't show up on time. After almost half an hour, Troy came to the restaurant."

"And?" Caitlyn's head pounded.

"I don't quite know how to tell you," Justin's dad said.

"Just say it." Caitlyn wasn't sure she wanted to hear what he had to say, but she needed to know.

His mother blurted out, "Justin is on a plane for New York."

"A plane?"

"We rushed to LAX and tried to stop him. Really, we did. But he wouldn't listen to reason," his dad said, anxiety evident in his voice.

"I don't understand what you're saying. Why would Justin fly to New York on the day of our wedding?" Her heart thumped in her ears. She felt her mother's arm around her shoulder.

Justin's mom let out a long sigh. "Caitlyn, Justin has gone to be with a girl he met while he was on his mission."

"A girl he met on his mission?" Caitlyn blinked her eyes several times and her mother's grip tightened.

"He's not coming back. He said to tell you he's sorry, but he couldn't go through with the wedding when he's . . ." her sentence trailed off.

"What?"

"In love with someone else," his father said.

The words sliced through her. She dropped the garment bag to the ground in a heap. Her perfect life was unraveling right before her. Intense sadness grasped her heart and squeezed it so tight she thought she might die on the spot.

"I'm so sorry, Caitlyn." His mom embraced her for a few moments.

"We didn't raise him to act this way. I don't know what's gotten into him. He has a lot of explaining to do," his father said.

Caitlyn stared at the ground. She'd been left at the altar, or as close to that as possible at the temple. How could he? Why didn't he say anything? He led her to believe he loved her and would marry her today. Now, she was standing in front of the temple, deserted. Her life was shattered. All of her planning, her dreaming, and her love was for nothing. She'd been abandoned on what was supposed to be the happiest day of her life.

"We'll take care of everything. We'll go in and speak with someone in the temple and call the caterer. We'll let the bishop know, and we'll make sure everyone gets the word before the reception was supposed to start. Don't worry about anything," Justin's father said. "It's the least we can do."

Caitlyn could hear Justin's mom crying.

"Thank you," Caitlyn's mom said. She whispered into Caitlyn's ear, "Let's get you back to the car."

Caitlyn sat in the backseat. She wasn't sure how she got there. She was numb, floating somewhere between dreaming and awakening.

"What kind of a young man does this?" her father said from the front seat.

"Robert, don't make her feel any worse. We don't need to discuss it right now," her mom said. "Let her work through this."

Lindsay reached over and caressed Caitlyn's hand. Caitlyn rested her head against the seat and stared out the window as they drove the freeway back toward Santa Barbara.

Today had not turned out at all like she had planned. She'd played it over and over again in her mind. How could Justin have fallen in love with another girl while he was supposed to be serving the Lord and while knowing that Caitlyn was home waiting for him? She wrapped her arms around herself, amazed at the physical pain she felt deep within her chest.

When they arrived home, Caitlyn went directly to her bedroom. She closed the door behind her and collapsed on her bed. She never wanted to leave her room. She'd cried so many tears on the way home, she didn't have any left. Her heart was smashed into a million pieces and her dreams were crushed. What about their apartment, their house on the mesa, their four children?

In the blink of an eye, or the takeoff of a plane, it was gone.

$$* \quad * \quad *$$

Several hours later, Caitlyn awoke to her mom standing in the doorway with a tray in her hands. "I'm sorry, I didn't mean to disturb you. I wanted to leave you a little something to eat." She placed the tray on the nightstand next to the bed.

Caitlyn wiped at her swollen eyes and sat up. She cleared her throat, "I'm not hungry."

"Maybe later."

Caitlyn shrugged.

"How are you feeling?"

"Sad. Confused."

"I'm so, so sorry, sweetheart."

Caitlyn nodded. She toppled back down on her bed and her mother snuggled up next to her.

"I can't believe he dumped me for another girl. Why didn't he tell me he didn't want to get married?"

"Maybe he was afraid."

"He fell in love with a girl on his mission. Who does that?"

"I don't know." Her mom brushed her hand against Caitlyn's cheek.

"What will I do now?"

"Go back to BYU."

"I can't. I told everyone about the wedding. Every time I have to answer why I'm not married, I'll have to relive the pain all over again. I can't do that. My heart hurts too much."

"People will understand."

"Will they? I don't even understand it." Tears snaked down her cheeks.

"In time you'll find someone else."

"No way. I never want to be hurt like this again. I'm done with marriage. Forever." She used her sleeve to wipe her eyes.

"You're still—"

"I trusted him. I believed him when he said we'd get married. Even though we couldn't see much of each other because I was at school when he got home from his mission, we talked on the phone and texted each other. He never said a word. When I came home to see him in October, he acted like we were still a couple. How could he change his mind like that? I don't understand."

"I don't know, honey, but your life will go on. I promise." Her mom stroked Caitlyn's hair. "I called your apartment office, and your contract hasn't sold, so you still have a place there."

"Mom, I can't go back. Not like this."

"You can, Cait. You can pick yourself up and go back."

"No. I can't."

"Even though this is something none of us expected, it will be a blessing."

"Right."

"Really. You'll see. Heavenly Father knows better than we do. It's far better that this happened now instead of after the marriage."

Caitlyn said nothing.

"You still have more than a week before school starts again.

Your dad said he'd take some time off work. We can all go to Provo and spend time together as a family before we drop you off."

Caitlyn closed her eyes. She desperately wished she'd wake up in the Bahamas, enjoying her honeymoon.

two

aitlyn twisted her hair into knots while she waited on a cold metal chair in the hallway at the Harris Fine Arts Center. She hadn't had time to straighten her naturally wavy hair this morning, and she was beginning to regret letting her roommate, Brittany, bleach it last week.

"Come on, Cait, you can't wallow in self pity for the rest of your life. You need a change, and I know exactly what to do," Brittany had said. The next thing she knew, she had electric yellow streaks throughout her hair. That was the last time she'd listen to Brittany.

Her heartbeat quickened, and her cheeks warmed. Why would the bishop want to speak with her? Sure, she'd been a hermit since she'd returned to school in January, but not for the reason Brittany thought. She was concentrating on school. Really. She didn't have time for a social life. That wasn't breaking any kind of a commandment. Maybe BYU was the premier breeding ground for eternally happy couples, but that wasn't for her. Nope. Justin had cured her of that. So why was she here?

The door creaked open, and a tall man with a dark suit and burgundy tie stepped out into the hall. He smiled and extended his hand. "Hello, Sister Moore."

Caitlyn stood, wiped her moist hands on her black skirt, and shook his hand. "Hello, Bishop." She half smiled.

"Ready for your talk in sacrament meeting?"

Caitlyn cleared her throat. "As ready as I'll ever be, I guess." She was counting down the seconds until the closing prayer.

"Thank you for waiting. Let's go into my office." Bishop Greene pushed the door open wider and gestured for Caitlyn to enter the small room that served as his office on Sundays. She sat in a padded chair opposite a small desk.

When Caitlyn first began attending BYU, she thought it strange that church meetings were held in buildings on campus. But after she realized how many wards served BYU students, it made sense. This year her ward met for sacrament meeting in the de Jong Concert Hall.

"What are you studying, Caitlyn?" Bishop Greene asked. He leaned back in his chair.

Caitlyn reached up and twirled her hair around her index finger. "I've been trying to get through my general ed. classes. But, I'm thinking about education. Maybe. Possibly. I don't know. No real plan anymore."

"Elementary or secondary?" Bishop Greene adjusted his dark-rimmed, bifocal glasses.

"Uh, I'm not sure. I'm taking an elementary education class this term." Caitlyn pulled her finger from the knot she'd made in her hair.

"My grandson teaches fifth grade. He earned his degree from BYU. It's an excellent program." Bishop Greene smiled.

Caitlyn shifted her weight in the vinyl-covered chair and inadvertently made a swooshy sound. She hoped Bishop Greene didn't think it was a rude body noise. She smoothed the wrinkles in her skirt and adjusted her pale pink shirt. She noticed how the light above the desk reflected off Bishop Greene's shiny bald head.

"I asked you to come in this morning because I'd like to extend a call."

Caitlyn's stomach somersaulted. A calling? What could she do to serve, especially in a student ward?

Bishop Greene leaned forward. "Would you be willing to serve as the mother of your family home evening group?"

Caitlyn swallowed hard. Mother? Of the family home evening group? She didn't even go to her FHE group. She'd sworn off anything remotely like a social situation. She coughed. "I don't know if I can do that. I'm so busy with school." It was true; she was busy, far too busy to be social.

"The Lord will qualify all who put their faith in Him. If you put your trust in the Lord, He will help you fulfill this calling and still accomplish all you need to for school. Do you believe that?" Bishop Greene peered at her.

She couldn't tell him that she had absolutely no desire to be part of any FHE group, especially if it meant she'd have to deal with guys. "Sure."

"Will you accept this calling?"

Her throat felt as though it was swelling shut. She didn't want to be rude by saying no, so she relented and said, "Yes, but I'm not sure what it means, exactly." She wiped her hands on her skirt again.

Bishop Greene nodded and said, "Not to worry. You can meet with the father of the group and coordinate with him. He's already accepted. Thank you, Sister Moore, for accepting this calling from the Lord."

Coordinate with *him?* That's all she needed, direct contact with a guy. Could she change her answer?

"His name is Travis Dixon."

"I don't think I know him." Caitlyn drew in a deep breath.

"He's recently moved into the ward, a nice-looking young man with dark hair. I'll make sure the two of you meet after sacrament meeting." Bishop Greene glanced at his watch. "Thank you again." He stood.

Caitlyn shook the bishop's hand and left his office. How could she maintain her hermit status now with this calling? All she needed was some jerk of a guy bugging her about FHE. She shook her head as she wandered down the corridor to the concert hall.

She found an empty chair on the stage and sat down. Her mind whirled from the call she'd been extended, and she still had her talk ahead of her. She gazed around the large room while it filled with familiar people.

Since she'd been living in the ward for the last nine months, she recognized almost everyone. She continued to survey the growing crowd. Hopefully, she wouldn't have to deal with this Travis guy very much.

The pianist stopped playing the prelude music sooner than Caitlyn had hoped, and Brother Conroy strolled over to the pulpit to begin the meeting. Caitlyn was still unsure about her new calling, but decided she'd have to get through it somehow.

Caitlyn noticed an unfamiliar face in the second-to-last row. That must be him. He had dark hair and a bright smile. She squinted, trying to take in more details, but then averted her eyes so it wasn't obvious she was looking him over. He had the typical "I'm-going-to-break-someone's-heart" kind of a face. Of course, all guys looked that way.

Throughout the meeting, she snuck glances in his direction hoping he wouldn't catch her. She wanted to size up her assistant in this new calling. After all, he'd need her to introduce him to everyone and take the lead. Maybe he'd stay out of her way, and it wouldn't be such a horrible experience.

"Our next speaker will be Sister Caitlyn Moore. After her remarks, we'll sing hymn number 156, *Sing We Now at Parting*, after which Sister Angie Patterson will offer the benediction." Brother Conroy sat down.

Caitlyn's chest tightened with each step toward the pulpit. Why did she have to speak on marriage of all things? Wasn't it enough that she'd been humiliated at the temple? Why pour lemon juice on a still open wound, especially since she'd vowed she'd never marry? Ever.

"Good morning, I think. I'd like to start my talk by turning to Doctrine and Covenants section 132."

Caitlyn continued to speak about celestial marriage for the next ten minutes. She read several scriptures and then concluded her talk. She walked back to her seat and sat down. Relief washed over her like the soft, foamy waves of the ocean back home. Marriage was fine for everyone else, but definitely not for her, and she didn't want to waste any more time thinking about something so unpredictable and daunting. She certainly didn't want Justin sneaking into her mind anymore.

After the meeting was over, the same guy from the second-to-last row made his way over to her. He stuck out his hand. "Nice talk."

Caitlyn shook his hand and said, "Thanks." She glanced up at him. He was a few inches taller than her and (though she tried not to notice) had deep blue eyes. The kind of eyes that made her forget her name. She swallowed hard.

"I'm Travis Dixon. I'm new in the ward. Just moved into Centennial II, apartment #12." He grinned.

"I'm . . ."

"Caitlyn. I heard Brother Conroy. I'm pretty good at picking up names mentioned over the pulpit." He grinned again, and she noticed his straight teeth.

"Yeah." Caitlyn's face flushed a bit.

"I hear we'll be serving together." His smiled widened.

"Yes, that's what I was told." She twirled her hair around her index finger.

"I've already let everyone know that we'll be meeting at my apartment later. Kind of a planning meeting."

"Oh, you have?" Caitlyn stiffened.

"See you about 6:00. And come with some fun ideas, no boring stuff allowed." He winked.

Caitlyn watched him saunter out of the room. She shook her head a few times. He seemed to be a bit pushy. After all, he'd moved into *her* ward, not the other way around. Besides, did she look boring?

"Great talk, Cait! I knew you could do it," Brittany said with a smirk.

"Thanks."

"Of course, no one knows what a whiner you were about doing it. Marriage isn't the worst thing that can happen, you know." Brittany braided her long, straight, auburn hair and secured it with a black rubber band.

"Yeah, it's the almost getting married part that's the worst." Caitlyn walked briskly out of the concert hall with Brittany right behind her.

"Who was that extremely hot guy you were talking to?" Brittany said over Caitlyn's shoulder.

"Travis Dixon."

Brittany caught up to Caitlyn. "New to the ward, huh? Fresh meat." She rubbed her hands together.

"You have a problem." Caitlyn shook her head.

"Just because I find guys attractive and haven't made a vow to lock myself in my room every night because some loser dumped me, doesn't mean I have a problem."

Caitlyn gave her a searing look.

"Come on, I'm kidding. Tell me what he was saying." Brittany reached out and pulled at Caitlyn's arm.

Caitlyn stopped and said, "I talked to the bishop between meetings."

"I wondered where you went during Sunday school."

"As if you noticed. You were pretty intent on talking to Garrett." Caitlyn fluttered her eyelids and fashioned a fake smile.

"Was not." Brittany pushed her.

"Were too. You never notice anything when you're flirting with Garrett." In a high, sing-songy voice Caitlyn said, "Oh, Garrett, you know so much about the scriptures. Maybe you'd come study them with me sometime? You're such a spiritual giant. Ooo, Garrett." Caitlyn made a kissing sound and then started walking again. Brittany grabbed her by the elbow.

"You're so making that up. I've never said anything like that to Garrett, even if it is true. And he's gorgeous, too. Whew!" Her brown eyes brightened.

Caitlyn pushed through the doors. They took a shortcut across campus. Caitlyn said nothing while Brittany talked nonstop about each and every guy in the ward. Finally, Brittany turned to Caitlyn and said, "You never told me what happened with the bishop or this new guy."

"I'm the new mom for our FHE group."

"That's so cool. Who's the dad? Oh, wait, let me guess. It's that Travis dude, huh?" Brittany moved her eyebrows up and down.

Caitlyn brushed past her roommate.

Brittany followed close behind. "He's hot. I can see it now." She lowered her voice and said, "You and Travis."

"Are you kidding me? I'm not at all interested in a guy like that, or any guy for that matter." They crossed Ninth East and walked down the sidewalk toward their apartment building.

"Oh, yeah, I forgot, you're going to devote yourself to your career . . . when you get one," Brittany said with a sarcastic tone.

"I don't remember asking your opinion."

"Justin was a loser, but that doesn't mean every guy is."

"Can we drop it? Do you have another clip? My hair is all over the place. I wish I had straight hair."

Brittany reached into her pocket, pulled out a silver barrette, and handed it to Caitlyn. "Gotta love those streaks, huh? You look good."

"Thanks." Caitlyn twisted her hair and clipped it to her head.

"Tell me what Travis said."

They continued walking along the sidewalk past other apartment buildings and condos.

"We're supposed to meet at his apartment at 6:00 today or something like that."

"And your problem is?"

"No problem." Caitlyn sped up.

"Yeah, right. I've been living with you long enough to know when someone has bugged you."

Caitlyn glanced up at the sky and then back at her roommate. "Why would he have bugged me? I hardly know the guy. Why would anything he do affect me in any way whatsoever?" Caitlyn emphasized her last statement with her hands.

Brittany stepped in front of Caitlyn, and they both came to a standstill in front of Gold's Gym. "I don't know, you tell me."

"You know," Caitlyn pointed her finger at Brittany, "you're starting to bug me." She stepped around Brittany and rushed toward their apartment complex.

"Fine, don't tell me, but I know there's something. I always know when there's something." Brittany called after her, "Oh, I know—you like him."

Caitlyn stopped and spun around. She rushed back. "What? I barely met the guy. I don't like him. That's ridiculous."

"Okay then, you're attracted to him," Brittany said.

"I think you've been out in the sun too long. Stop going to the pool; the sun's damaged your brain." Caitlyn flicked Brittany on the head, turned around, and darted toward their apartment, leaving Brittany in the street.

three

Caitlyn hurried up the steps to her apartment. She opened the door and immediately recognized the stench of dirty dishes. She walked past the living room and into her bedroom. The pile of clothes in the corner of her room indicated that she had an upcoming date in the laundry room. She rifled through the pile and found her favorite gray sweat pants and a bright orange T-shirt with her high school tennis team's logo on it. She paused to gaze at herself in the crooked mirror that hung on the wall.

Although she hated to admit it, Brittany was right about one thing. Travis had affected her. Somehow, in the brief moments she talked to him, he'd gotten to her, and she didn't like it. She wasn't ready for anyone to get to her, not yet. Make that not ever. She shook her head and walked into the kitchen.

She ignored the dishes in the sink and filled her water bottle. She flopped onto the couch, pulled out her cell phone, and speed-dialed her home number.

"Hello?" came the familiar voice.

"Hey, Linds."

"Hi, Cait."

"How's school going?"

"Don't even ask." Lindsay let out a grunt.

"That bad, huh? Cheer up, it's almost over this year and then you'll be a senior. Senior year rocks."

"How's the Y and all the guys?" Lindsay asked.

"School's good. It's finally warmed up enough for some pool time. I definitely need a tan, though. I can't come home and go to the beach looking like a ghost. Is Mom home?"

"She's trying to grab the phone from me. See ya, Cait."

"Mom?"

"Hello, Caitlyn. How are you?"

"I'm fine, Mom, really." She licked her lips. She knew exactly what her mom meant, and she fought to keep her resentment in check.

"You know—"

"Yes, yes, I know. He got married yesterday. So what? I've been over Justin for a long, long time. In fact, it's been so long, it's almost been infinity." Caitlyn tapped her fingers on the small table next to the couch.

"I hope you don't mind, but I went to the reception. She seems like a nice girl, but not as nice as you, of course." Her mom sounded sincere.

Caitlyn's stomach tightened, and she gripped the phone as the razor-sharp memory replayed in her mind. "I'm glad you went," she lied.

"Are you sure?"

"Yes. I hope Justin's happy." She tried to keep the sarcastic tone out of her voice.

"How was church today?"

"I spoke in sacrament meeting, and I got a calling. I'm the mom of my family home evening group."

"You are?" Her mother sounded proud.

"The guy that's serving as the dad is pretty annoying," Caitlyn said as she rolled her eyes.

"I hope you have a good week, honey. I miss you."

"I miss you, too. Is Dad home?"

"He's playing golf today."

"Did he let the missionaries come over yet?"

"No." Caitlyn could hear the disappointment in her mom's voice.

"I thought he said they could come over for dinner."

"He changed his mind, and I'm not going to push him."

"I wish—"

"I do, too. I'll tell him you called. I love you, Caitlyn."

"Love you, too, Mom." She hung up the phone and took a swig from her water bottle. She leaned her head back. If only her dad wouldn't be so stubborn.

And, if anyone cared, she was over Justin. Really. In fact, she was over all guys—permanently.

The door flung open. "Whew, that Garrett is one hot guy, I tell you what." Brittany threw herself on the couch, bumping into Caitlyn.

"Did he ask you out?"

"I think he was about to when Tara interrupted us."

"How inconvenient. She is his girlfriend, you know." Caitlyn slapped Brittany on the shoulder.

"Minor complication, that's all. A guy as hot as he is deserves someone like me, at least for a few dates." Brittany puckered up her lips.

Caitlyn shook her head.

*   *   *

"It's 6:00. Let's go," Caitlyn said.

"I'm coming," Brittany yelled down the hall.

"Have you seen Hannah?" Caitlyn called back.

"Are you kidding? She and what's-his-name are probably over at his apartment, like usual. Are they engaged yet?"

"That'd be a big mistake," Caitlyn muttered under her breath.

Brittany came bounding out of her bedroom. "I'm ready." She made a siren noise. "Ooo, fashion emergency. You aren't wearing those sweats and that hideous T-shirt, are you? You might have been a tennis champ back in high school, but fashion?"

"Excuse me?" Caitlyn placed her hands on her hips.

"You look like a slob."

"So? We're going over for a planning meeting. No big deal. Besides, these are my favorite sweats." Caitlyn rubbed her hands up and down her legs.

"Obviously. It looks like you've loved them a bit too much." Brittany crinkled her nose.

"I'm not trying to impress anyone." She was proud of her freedom-from-social-expectations attitude.

"Then you're dressed appropriately," Brittany said.

"Let's go, we'll be late." Caitlyn grabbed Brittany's arm. "I want to get this over with as fast as possible."

"You're such a hermit."

"And proud of it."

Caitlyn took the steps two at a time up to Travis's apartment. She knocked on the door while Brittany climbed the stairs.

The door swung open, and Travis stood in the doorway. "Hello, ladies, please come in." He bowed.

"What a gentleman," Brittany whispered in Caitlyn's ear.

"Uh-huh," said Caitlyn. What a show-off. And his cowboy boots? Lame. Disdain welled up in her throat and threatened to explode all over him. She swallowed it back down.

Caitlyn, with arms folded across her chest, leaned against the counter in the kitchen. She glanced around. The kitchen was immaculate, not a single dish in the sink. The counters housed nothing but a pack of photos. She reached over and gently rummaged through the pictures. It looked like they were taken at some sort of camping trip. She didn't recognize anyone but Travis in the group photos. She noticed a girl with long, stringy, brown hair hanging on Travis in almost every picture. Probably a sister.

"I called you all here so we could do some planning for FHE. We'll need to get everyone's ideas. Let's have a prayer and get started," Travis said as he stood in the middle of the group.

After the prayer, a girl with short red hair whom Caitlyn didn't recognize said, "How about a barbecue? We can grill hamburgers at a park in Provo Canyon."

"What does everyone think about that?" Travis said.

Most of the people nodded their heads in agreement.

"And what does our mother think?" Travis tipped his head toward Caitlyn.

"Whatever." She shrugged her shoulders and refused to meet his gaze. Just because she was the mom of the FHE group didn't mean she had to participate, so it didn't matter what they decided to do.

"Any other ideas?" Travis glanced around the room.

"Game night," said Ethan, a short, skinny guy with a receding hairline.

"A movie at the cheap theater," Alexis shouted out.

"Let's go hiking," said Bruce whose thick black hair always looked like he'd rolled out of bed.

"The girls could make dinner for the guys," said Jake, Bruce's extra-tall roommate.

All of the girls booed, and Brittany slugged him in the arm.

Everyone started talking to each other. Travis stepped over to Caitlyn and above the chatter of the group, he said, "Let's write this down." He handed her a pen and a paper.

Caitlyn took them grudgingly. Did he think she was his personal secretary or something?

"We can do a cookout. Write that down for next week. We'll eat Frank."

"Excuse me?"

"We can eat Frank. He's in the freezer," Travis said with a smirk.

"Frank? In the freezer?" Caitlyn said in a high voice.

"Yeah. We butchered him a few months ago. He'll taste good." Travis smacked his lips together. "Makes my mouth water thinking about it."

"What are you, a mass murderer?" Caitlyn took a step back, feeling a little uneasy.

Travis gave her a look that made her feel as though she'd grown another head. "Frank was one of my best steers."

"A what?"

"A boy cow that wasn't a boy anymore, to be exact."

Caitlyn held up her hands. "Eeww. Too much information."

"My family raises cattle. I have my own small herd." Travis grinned, seeming to enjoy himself at her expense.

"I see. You actually name your cows?"

"Sure. It's easier to keep track of them that way. Of course, it's hard to name 'em all if you have three hundred head or so. But Grandpa names the meanest and stubbornnest ones; they're the first to get butchered." He laughed.

"Serious?" Caitlyn's eyes widened and a sick feeling hit her stomach.

"Absolutely."

"I've never met a cowboy. Although, I've seen a John Wayne movie. Does that count?" Caitlyn raised her eyebrow.

"I don't think so. Maybe one of these days you'll come see a real, live cowboy ranch."

Was that some sort of an invitation? Why would she be interested in seeing a ranch, especially if it meant being with him? Arrogance, pure and simple. And how did he suck her into a conversation?

He sat down and leaned back in his chair. "Where are you from, Mom?"

"Let's go bowling," Ethan yelled out to Travis.

"Sounds good," Travis answered. "Put that down in a couple of weeks."

Caitlyn scrawled bowling on the calendar for the last Monday in May. "I'm from Santa Barbara. That's a city in southern California."

"Makes sense." Travis said it with a bit of smugness.

"What's that supposed to mean?" Caitlyn sat on the edge of the coffee table.

"City girl."

"Is there something wrong with that?" Caitlyn placed her hands on her hips, becoming more annoyed with him. He was getting under her skin, and she was done with the conversation.

"Nope. Not a thing." Travis shook his head.

"Maybe we should get back to planning the calendar." Caitlyn pushed the paper toward Travis.

Brittany interrupted their conversation. "Alexis had a great idea for an activity in June—"

"Caitlyn will write it down." Travis glanced at his watch. "Uh-oh. I didn't realize it was so late." He looked directly at Caitlyn and said, "We'll have to finish this tomorrow night after family home evening."

The tone in his voice irritated Caitlyn. She wanted to find the nearest pillow and pummel him with it. There was nothing wrong with being a city girl. Besides, who had ever heard of naming a cow and then eating it anyway? It was disgusting. And did he think she was there to serve his every whim? Maybe she had plans after FHE.

No doubt about it, this was going to be a long, long spring term.

four

"Your dinner date is here, Alison," Alison's roommate, Jessica, yelled down the hall.

"Can you let him in on your way out? I have a few finishing touches. Thanks," Alison said, excitement wrapping around her.

Alison looked in the mirror and applied another coat of lip gloss. She brushed through her long brown hair, and then picked up a bottle of perfume. She sprayed her wrist and the front of her neck. "Perfect," she said. She raised her shoulders a bit and grinned at herself in the mirror.

She meandered down the hallway and entered the living room with the cloud of perfume behind her.

"Hi, Trav."

Travis stood up. "Hey, Alison. Something sure smells good."

With a coy smile, Alison softly said, "You think so?"

"Is it chicken or pork?"

"Huh?"

"Dinner."

"Oh, that." Alison reassessed the situation and without missing a beat, she said, "It's beef. I know that's your favorite. And this is a roast from one of Daddy's very best steers. He grain-fed him all winter to get the most tender meat. Mom gave me a few of the best cuts when I was home a few weeks ago. I saved this one for you."

She eyed Travis and willed her heart to slow down.

Travis looked even better than she'd ever seen him, with his thick dark hair that screamed for her to run her fingers through it. And his mesmerizing eyes. His jeans hugged all the right places, and his sexy cowboy boots made her feel woozy. They'd have beautiful children together, that was for sure.

"You're making my mouth water."

"You feel it, too?" She stepped close to him.

Travis gave her a look. "What?"

"Oh, the food." She cleared her throat and stepped back. "I've made garlic mashed potatoes, homemade rolls, a green salad with your favorite dressing, and a cherry cheesecake for dessert." She smiled, took his hand, and led him to the dinner table.

"You spoil me." Travis took his seat.

"Tell me you don't love it." She looked deep into his eyes and was sure she could stay there forever.

Travis gazed around the table, impeccably set with a bouquet of flowers that graced the center. "Looks delicious."

"Aren't you glad you came?"

"A homemade dinner instead of Top Ramen? I'd say so." He patted her on the back, and she leaned into him.

After the blessing, Alison served Travis a plate overflowing with food. She pulled her chair close to his.

"Thanks for inviting me for dinner." Travis took a bite of salad.

"I haven't seen you for a week or so, and I missed you. Did you miss me?" She made doe eyes.

"I'm sorry; I've been busy with work."

"At Albertsons?"

Travis nodded and lifted his fork with a piece of roast on it. He slipped it into his mouth. "Mmmm. This is so good. It may even rival my mom's roast, but don't tell her I said so."

Alison raised her finger to her mouth. "My lips are sealed. I'm glad you like it." She knew how he loved a good meal and hoped he'd see that she'd make a wonderful wife.

Travis turned to her. "What have you been up to?"

"Working at the hospital in Orem."

"Congratulations on getting your nursing degree. That's awesome."

"I set it as a goal and, as my mom keeps telling me, once my mind is made up, nothing gets in my way." She touched Travis on the shoulder. "Nursing is good, but my real goal is to get married and have lots of kids."

"Have you heard from Spencer?"

Alison sat back against her chair. "Yeah. He's a district leader now and loves Germany."

"I can't believe your little brother is on his mission already."

"Time goes by fast. We shouldn't waste any of it." Alison moved in closer to Travis again.

Travis sipped his milk and took another bite of the mashed potatoes.

"I talked to Tanya the other day." Alison smiled.

"Yeah?"

"She's my best friend, you know. She's anxious to come back to school. We're going to live together in the fall, unless, of course, something changes." Alison looked at Travis from the corner of her eye hoping he'd understand what she meant.

Travis cocked his head. "Are you thinking about leaving Provo?"

"Oh, no, I'm not going anywhere. I'll be here all summer and into the fall, unless . . ."

"That's my plan, too. I'm hoping to have enough money saved to start school this fall."

They continued to visit, and when Travis finished his dinner, Alison served him an extra large piece of cherry cheesecake. After dessert they moved to the small couch.

"Jessica, my new roommate, won't be home for hours. We could find a movie to watch or something."

"I've got to get up early in the morning. I should probably head home."

"But . . ." Her sentence trailed off.

"Dinner was great. Thank you. It hit the spot." Travis stood.

29

Alison jumped to her feet. "I was hoping you'd stay a little longer. Did you happen to bring back my photos?"

Travis hit himself on the forehead. "I'm sorry. I forgot them back at the apartment. We had an FHE gathering, and it slipped my mind. I'll drop them by this week."

"How about tomorrow night?"

"My FHE group is meeting for shakes."

"You could come by afterward, and we could catch a late movie or talk."

"I'll see what I can do."

Did she have to hit him over the head or what? He was so oblivious to her hints. She brightened and said, "Maybe I could meet up with you at your apartment and go with you to get a shake."

"That'd be great, but I was just called to my new position as FHE dad, and tomorrow night is our first official activity."

Alison waved her hand. "That's cool." She forced a smile. Was he being difficult on purpose or totally dense?

"Thanks again for dinner." Travis stepped over to the door.

Alison leaned in, hoping he'd kiss her, but he opened the door instead. She took a step back and said, "Thanks for coming over. I'll see you soon?"

"Sure."

Alison closed the door and fell to the floor in a pile of frustration. What was wrong with him? She didn't expect him to propose exactly, but at least a kiss to let her know they were back on track toward a lasting relationship. It definitely hadn't gone according to her and Tanya's plan.

It was time to speed things up with Travis. They'd dated on and off long enough. The summer after their senior year, when they made the trip to the State Fair in Pueblo, she determined to be Mrs. Travis Dixon. They both loved animals and agriculture, and she wanted nothing more than to live on a ranch back home in Colorado, raising a bunch of kids with Travis.

Tonight was a misstep in the plan, but no matter, eventually they'd end up at the Manti Temple with her flowing white dress, six bride's maids dressed in baby blue, and a bouquet of yellow roses.

five

"I don't care what you say. Travis is way hot," Brittany said. She flung her legs over the side of the couch in their apartment.

"Whatever," Caitlyn answered.

"You two seemed to be hitting it off." Brittany grabbed an old piece of popcorn she found among the cushions and threw it into the air attempting to catch it in her mouth. It bounced off her nose and hit the floor.

"That's attractive. And we weren't hitting it off. Far from it." Caitlyn stretched out across the carpeted floor feeling nothing but dislike for her FHE spouse.

"What's the problem?" Brittany again picked up the popcorn and threw it in the air. This time it landed in her mouth.

Caitlyn gave her a look and said, "Hmm, let's see. First, he took over the whole group and told everyone to meet at his apartment."

"So?"

"This is my ward." Caitlyn pointed to herself. "He moved into it. He's acting like it's his ward."

"Isn't it?"

Caitlyn gave Brittany another look. "Whose side are you on?"

"I didn't know we were taking sides."

Caitlyn squinted her eyes. "Then, at his apartment, he was bossing me around and treating me like I was his secretary. And, to top it off, he acted like being from the city was some sort of sin."

"Did he say that?"

"He didn't have to." Caitlyn rolled over on her stomach, irritation boiling up.

"Uh-huh."

"What?" Caitlyn propped her head up on her hands

"I see what's going on here." Brittany sat up on the couch.

"You do?"

"You like him."

"Not a chance. No way. Not even slightly." She was becoming annoyed with Brittany.

"You're proving my point right now." Brittany giggled.

"I'm not talking about this anymore." Caitlyn rolled over to her back, sat up, and jumped to her feet.

"This is good."

Caitlyn walked over to the refrigerator and rummaged through it. She found a pickle jar and pulled it out. She opened it and dipped her fingers in to catch a floating pickle.

"Finally, someone to take your mind off Justin. You've been moping around this apartment ever since you got back from Christmas break. And the last few weeks have been even worse."

Caitlyn replaced the jar inside the refrigerator and slammed the door shut, making jars rattle inside it.

"You said you were over him, but not until today have I seen any evidence of that. It's about time, too. Four months is long enough to mourn. You need to get on with your life."

Caitlyn walked back into the living room with a pickle in her hand and flopped down on the love seat. Her mouth puckered as the sour taste hit her tongue.

"Travis is the first guy that's gotten any kind of reaction out of you," Brittany said. "I finally see hope for you."

"It never even crossed my mind that Justin would dump me—"

"When a door closes . . ."

"It crushes you into bits." Caitlyn took another bite of her pickle, and juice dribbled down her chin. She wiped at it with the back of her hand.

"No. A window opens."

"I don't even know what that means." Caitlyn shoved the rest of the pickle in her mouth.

"There's someone else for you." Brittany picked up a pillow and threw it at Caitlyn.

"Not interested."

"I don't believe you."

"Believe what you want. I'm going to concentrate on school and that's all," Caitlyn said. She didn't care what Brittany said. She definitely wasn't interested in dating anyone, especially Travis.

Someone knocked at the door. "I wonder who that is. Maybe it's Garrett. Or better yet, maybe it's Travis," Brittany said, rubbing her hands together. She jumped up and rushed to the door.

Caitlyn's heartbeat quickened, and her face warmed. It couldn't be Travis at the door, could it? Even if it was, she didn't care. Right? Just in case, though, she darted down the hall and ducked into the bathroom.

"Oh, hi, Chase. How's it going?" Brittany said in a loud voice.

Caitlyn let out a breath of relief that it wasn't Travis. She stood still listening for Chase's reply. "Is Caitlyn home?"

"Uh, yeah, but . . ."

"Do you think she'd like to go out this weekend?" It seemed like the question exploded out of his mouth.

Caitlyn leaned against the bathroom wall, holding her breath. Chase was a nice guy. He was even decent-looking with his bright blond hair and hazel eyes, but he wasn't date material, at least not for her. No one was.

"Umm . . ." Brittany said, leaving it hanging in the air.

Caitlyn quietly shut the bathroom door and quickly turned on the water to the shower. She hoped Brittany would take the cue.

After a few moments, Brittany threw open the door to the bathroom. "What is wrong with you?"

"I don't want to go out with him."

"Why not? He's a nice guy. He's attractive, too."

"Did you hear a word I said? I'm not interested in dating anyone." Caitlyn shut off the water.

"He said he'd come back over to ask you out."

"You should go out with him. Isn't he one of the only guys you haven't dated in the ward?"

"And Travis. At least, not yet." Brittany turned around and sauntered out.

"What's that supposed to mean?"

"I guess if you're not going to go after Travis, then he's fair game."

"I don't care if you date Travis. Have him—he's all yours. I'm not interested in Travis." Caitlyn emphasized her last sentence.

"Cool. I can fit him in between Garrett and this new guy, Jordan, I met at the library." She turned to Caitlyn. "Aren't you ever going to date anyone?"

"No. I can be completely happy on my own. Then I don't have to worry about having my heart ripped out, stomped on, shredded to a pulp, and thrown back at me. Besides, not everyone wants to be a dating queen."

"I'm not the one that's so scared of getting hurt again that I hide in the bathroom at the mere mention of a date."

Caitlyn shook her head. "I'm going to bed."

"Pleasant dreams." Brittany gave her a little wave, and Caitlyn rolled her eyes.

Caitlyn lay in bed thinking about her conversation with Brittany when images of Travis seeped in. She placed her pillow over her face, hoping to snuff out any thought of Travis.

Without warning, Justin popped into her mind. Time had healed the sharp, stabbing pain she'd first felt when he left her at the temple doors, but it had reemerged during winter semester when she found out about Justin's upcoming marriage plans to that girl from his mission.

It was then that Caitlyn decided she'd attend spring term and possibly stay in Provo through the summer. She couldn't bear to face Justin and his new wife while they lived the life she'd planned.

She rolled to her side. She'd be happy on her own. Without Justin. And certainly without that Travis guy.

six

"It's a warm spring day here in Utah Valley this morning," said the woman's grating voice on the radio. Caitlyn reached over and slapped it off. It had been a short night, and she wasn't ready to start the day.

"Are you awake?" Brittany said through the door.

Caitlyn pulled the hair from in front of her eyes and cleared her throat. "As far as I know."

Brittany opened the door and tossed Caitlyn her cell phone.

"Who is it?" Caitlyn mouthed.

Brittany smiled and turned around.

Caitlyn cleared her throat again. "Hello?"

"Caitlyn?"

"Yes?"

"It's Travis Dixon."

Caitlyn dropped the phone and then quickly picked it up. "Hi, Travis." Why did his voice make her nerves flutter? And how did he get her number?

"I wanted to make sure we were all meeting at the Shake Shoppe tonight for FHE."

"Isn't that what we decided yesterday?" Caitlyn fought off a yawn.

"Did I wake you?"

"Oh, no, I've been up for hours." She pulled at her hair and wiped at her mouth

"Good. I keep forgetting not everyone lives ranch hours. Glad to know you're an early riser."

"Of course," she said, not wanting him to know she rarely left bed before 10:00 a.m. if she had her choice.

"Well, then, I'll be at your apartment at 6:45 tonight," he said.

"Are we meeting here?" She sat up in her bed.

"No. I thought I'd walk over there with you."

"Oh." Her palms began to perspire, and despite her best effort to conceal a smile, it peeked out around the corners of her mouth.

"Is that a problem?" He sounded sincere.

She reached up and twirled a lock of hair around her index finger. "No problem. That'll be fine."

"See you then. Bye."

Caitlyn closed her phone. "You might as well come in," she shouted.

The door opened slightly. "I was walking past—"

"You so had your ear up against the door. Don't even deny it."

Brittany took a few steps and landed at the end of Caitlyn's bed. "So?"

"What?"

"Details."

"Wipe that ridiculous smile off your face first."

"Tell me what he said." Brittany clapped her hands together.

"You're so nosey."

"Call me whatever you want, but tell me what he said."

"He wants to walk us over to the Shake Shoppe, that's all. He didn't profess his undying love for me or ask me to elope to the Hawaii Temple."

"He said *us?*" Brittany emphasized the last word.

Caitlyn nodded.

"You're such a liar."

"Am not." Caitlyn maintained a serious expression.

"He likes you. Admit it." Brittany pushed Caitlyn over.

"Until yesterday he never even knew I existed. He's fulfilling his calling, that's all. What do I have to do to prove I'm not interested in this hick farmer?"

"Is that why your eyes are dancing?" Brittany asked with a smirk.

"Dancing? That's the dumbest thing you've ever said and that's saying something." Caitlyn fluttered her eyelids.

"I'm right." Brittany jumped up. "See you tonight." She skipped out of the room.

"Dancing? That's ridiculous. She's crazy," Caitlyn said to herself as she glanced across the room into the mirror that hung on the wall.

Dancing?

*　　*　　*

"It's 6:30. Cait, are you ready?" Brittany's voice carried through the apartment.

"Almost."

"You take forever in the bathroom," Brittany said from the living room.

"Hang on! I'll be out in a second." Caitlyn examined herself in the mirror and checked out her crisp khaki Capris and off-white print T-shirt.

"New outfit?" Brittany looked her up and down.

"My mom sent it to me the other day. I think she's trying to ease my pain over Justin's wedding. Do you like it?" Caitlyn twirled around a few times.

"Looks good. Any particular reason you decided to wear it tonight?" Brittany winked.

"Nope. I haven't had a chance to wear it yet, that's all. And stop winking. You look like you have some weird tick or something." Caitlyn cleared her throat and said, "Where's Hannah?"

"I haven't seen her in days."

"She still lives here, doesn't she?"

Brittany shrugged. "I bet she and Dave are engaged or close to it."

"I hope not." Caitlyn put a piece of gum in her mouth.

"So no one should get married?"

Caitlyn gave Brittany a look. "Because they can't get married in the temple."

"Oh, well, yeah."

"We live in the fertile valley of RMs, and she finds a nonmember."

"He's a nice guy, though. I guess that's something." Brittany fluffed her hair.

"Nice guy or not, he can't take her to the temple."

"I didn't think you felt that strong about the temple because—"

"Of Justin?"

"No. Your dad."

"That's exactly why I think temple marriage is so important—"

Rhythmic beating on the front door interrupted their conversation.

"Must be Travis." Brittany moved her eyebrows up and down. She turned around and sashayed toward the door. Caitlyn followed her, trying to regulate her breathing and chastising herself for feeling so nervous.

Brittany opened the door. Travis stood there in a light blue T-shirt, jeans, and cowboy boots. Caitlyn noticed his broad shoulders and well-defined biceps. She attempted to squelch the inconvenient butterflies tickling her stomach.

"Hello, ladies." He smiled, and Caitlyn's heart momentarily stopped.

"Thank you ever so much for being so gallant and walking us over to The Shake Shoppe," Caitlyn said in a mock southern accent hoping it would hide her anxiety.

"No problem. These mean city streets can be a might bit dangerous for such lovely young ladies," Travis said with a matching drawl.

Brittany looked between Travis and Caitlyn. "Hey, there's Amanda and Carrie. I'm going to walk with them if you don't mind," Brittany said with an innocent smile that Caitlyn recognized as anything but.

Caitlyn watched her roommate rush over to the girls that lived in the apartment next door.

"I guess that leaves the two of us," Travis said. He smiled. How did he keep his teeth so white? She reprimanded herself for even noticing because she absolutely was not interested in dating anyone. Really.

"Guess so." Caitlyn closed the door behind them.

The spring air cooled as they walked through the parking lot and down the street toward the Shake Shoppe.

"Santa Barbara, huh?"

"Yeah. Born and raised." Caitlyn placed her hands in her pockets.

"I had a missionary companion from Oxnard. I didn't believe that there was actually a place called Oxnard. It sounds like something that'd come out of a cow's nose." He held up his hand and said, "Careful there, don't step in that ox-nard." He stepped to the side.

Caitlyn laughed. She hadn't thought of it before, but the name did sound funny. She started to feel more at ease. "Where did you serve your mission?"

"Brazil."

"How was it?" What a dumb question.

Travis lit up. "It was the hardest thing I've ever done in my life, but I loved it. It's a whole different world there." He seemed lost in his thoughts.

Caitlyn looked over at him and saw the sparkle in his eyes. Maybe he wasn't as obnoxious as he'd seemed yesterday. Before she realized it, they were at The Shake Shoppe. "What's your favorite kind of shake?" Travis asked.

"Anything chocolate."

"I see. A chocoholic. I've been surrounded by them my whole life. I think my sister went in for treatment for her chocolate addiction." He grinned, and Caitlyn exerted all of her effort to not let it affect her.

"Hey, Caitlyn," Chase said as he moved close to her.

"Hi, Chase."

Chase stepped in between Caitlyn and Travis. "I was thinking maybe this weekend, you'd like to—"

Chase stopped his sentence when he involuntarily stepped forward and lost his grip on his shake.

"Sorry, dude, I didn't mean to bump into you like that. And I've spilled your shake." Travis grabbed a couple of napkins and handed them to Chase.

"Thanks," Chase said. He wiped at his chest.

Caitlyn tried to hold it in, but a giggle escaped her lips.

"So, Caitlyn—" Chase started again.

"Next, please," said a young woman working behind the counter.

"She'll have to get back to you. She needs to order her shake," Travis said. He gently pushed Caitlyn toward the counter.

"Talk to you later, I guess." Chase walked off with a look of dejection on his face.

"What can I get you?" asked the young woman.

"I think I'd like a Triple Chocolate Lovers Delight, please," Caitlyn said.

"I'll have the same."

"So, your sister isn't the only chocoholic in the family?"

"No comment." Travis looked straight ahead.

They both grabbed their shakes and walked outside. Caitlyn noticed Chase walking toward her.

"Let's get everyone and go back to my apartment. You go over there, and I'll get this group here." Travis guided Caitlyn in the opposite direction of Chase.

They all cut through the parking lot next to the strip mall and headed toward the apartment complex. Brittany smirked at Caitlyn a few times, but Caitlyn ignored her.

At the apartment, Travis said, "Let's play a game."

Most of the group nodded in agreement. Travis pulled out a chair for Caitlyn to sit down. It was across the room from Chase. Caitlyn wasn't quite sure what was happening.

"We'll start by pulling questions out of this paper bag. I'll go first." Travis reached his hand into the bag and pulled out a small white paper. "How many siblings do you have and what are their names? I have a twin sister named Tanya, a younger brother Greg, who's on a mission, and three younger sisters, Shanna, Julie, and Dawn. Who's next? Mom?"

Caitlyn turned and saw his grin. Her stomach flip-flopped. "Sure." She reached her hand into the bag and pulled out a paper. She read, "What's your most embarrassing moment?"

Laughter filled the room. Caitlyn swallowed hard and blinked her eyes several times as memories of her almost marriage paraded through her mind.

"I don't think so." She handed the paper back to Travis.

"Why not?" Travis said.

"You get to name your brothers and sisters, and I have to come up with my most embarrassing moment? No way. You planted that. I want another one."

"Okay, go ahead." She noticed Travis still wore a silly grin.

She read the next one. "What's your most embarrassing moment?" She threw the paper at Travis. "What is this?"

"I made up the game and all of the questions . . ."

Caitlyn yanked the bag out of his hands and pulled out the papers. They all said the same thing.

"Excuse me?"

"I thought it'd be fun to hear about everyone's most embarrassing moments, starting with you." He laughed.

"No way."

"Oh, come on, Cait, you can tell us about the time you made cookies for the bishop and used a cup of salt instead of sugar," Brittany shouted from the back of the group.

A few people groaned.

"So I'm not a cook." She raised her hands above her head. She turned to Travis and said, "Go ahead, Dad, you take a turn on this one."

"No problem. It was when I was a freshman at the dorms." Travis became animated while he shared his story. "I was taking a shower and my roommate swiped all of my clothes. When I got out of the shower, I realized what'd happened so I ran down the hall in my birthday suit. When I got to my door, it was locked, of course. So, I went back to the bathroom." He mimicked taking light steps and looked from side to side. "I wasn't sure what to do, so I thought about it for a minute." He tapped his forehead.

"I could see my open dorm window from the bathroom and figured I could dive into it from the bathroom window." Several girls gasped and covered their mouths. The guys in the room were laughing.

Travis continued, "I made sure the coast was clear and dove into my room."

"How embarrassing," said one of the girls.

Travis nodded. "After I got into my room, I heard clapping. I looked outside, and there stood my roommate and several people he'd gathered to watch me make my escape."

"You're making that up," Caitlyn said.

"No, no, I wish I were. I couldn't face anyone for the rest of that day."

"Probably wouldn't recognize your face," Chase said in a loud voice. The whole group erupted in laughter.

When Caitlyn finally stopped laughing, she said, "You deserved that."

Travis turned to her and, with his arm extended, said, "Now, it's your turn. And make it a little more embarrassing than rock hard cookies."

"I think you've provided us with more than enough entertainment for the evening. Wouldn't you all agree?" she said to the group.

They closed their FHE with a prayer and everyone started filing through the apartment door. Most were still laughing at Travis's story.

"I seem to have lost my roommate." Caitlyn glanced around the apartment.

"Brittany?" Travis said.

"Yeah."

"Was your other roommate here?" he asked.

"Hannah? No. She's got a serious boyfriend, so we hardly ever see her."

"I'd be happy to walk you home." Travis took a step through the doorway.

Caitlyn held up her hand. "You don't have to do that. I'm sure I'll find Brit along the way. She'll be flirting with every guy from here to our apartment."

"I'd like to walk you home, if that's okay." Travis tipped his head, and a tickling sensation filled her stomach.

Trying to control her excitement, she said, "Why not? Maybe you can share some more of your dorm experiences."

Across the patio area, Caitlyn saw Chase and waved. Travis kept tight to her side as they ascended the stairs to her apartment.

Travis opened the front door for Caitlyn, stepped inside after her, and closed the door behind him.

"Would you like to sit down?" Caitlyn asked after Travis sat on the couch.

He smiled and leaned back.

"Want a drink?"

"Don't mind if I do."

Caitlyn searched through the refrigerator. She was certain she could find something to drink. She pushed aside the mold-infested dish of something that resembled a dinner they'd had a few weeks earlier. She found a couple of shriveled apples and some wilted lettuce. She eyed the jar of pickle juice, but decided against serving that as a beverage.

"Hmm, let's see. What about a glass of water? I know we have that," Caitlyn said over the top of the refrigerator door.

"Sounds good."

The front door swung open and Brittany fell in. "Oops, sorry, I didn't know we had company. Hi, Travis, or should I call you Dad?"

"Travis is fine."

"That was quite a story you told." Brittany laughed.

"Every word of it was true, Scout's honor." Travis raised his hand and gave the Scout sign.

"I'd like to meet your roommate. Tall guy with sandy blond hair, pale blue eyes, great body," Brittany said.

"Darren. I'll see what I can arrange." Travis smiled.

"Maybe the four of us could get together?" Brittany said.

"Uh, Brit, you forgot your cell phone and it's been beeping. Must be a voice mail for you. Better call right away." Caitlyn planted the phone in Brittany's hand and shoved her down the hall.

"Brittany has a good idea," Travis said.

"What?" Caitlyn sat on the chair next to the couch.

"How about a movie tomorrow night? We can bring Brittany and Darren along, too." Travis sat up and leaned toward the front of the couch.

A date? "I've got tons of homework I need to do." Caitlyn took a sip of her water, hoping it would settle her nerves, and she could avoid making a date.

Travis gave her a puppy dog look.

"I guess I shouldn't turn down someone who's bared his soul, among other things," Caitlyn said before she could stop herself.

"We'll be by to pick you up about 6:30 then."

"Okay." Caitlyn took another sip of her water and then set it on the small, imitation wood table.

"Let Brittany know, would you?" Travis stood up. "I better get back. I'll see you tomorrow night." Travis stepped over to the front door, opened it, and walked out.

Caitlyn stood in the doorway and leaned against the doorframe. What was he doing to her? She felt an eagerness that she hadn't felt since Justin. She wanted to spend time with Travis, but couldn't explain why. After all, he was annoying and bossy and pushy and, well, more things that she was sure would make it impossible to date him. And she knew better than anyone that nothing good could come from dating, only heartbreak. Yet . . .

Brittany bounded down the hall. "What's up?"

"Your little plan worked." Caitlyn shut the door.

"Plan?" Brittany jumped on the couch and sat on her feet.

"To get Travis to ask me out." Caitlyn sat on the ground. "I said no."

"But it's so obvious there's chemistry between you."

Caitlyn snapped her head up. "Chemistry? You've been watching too many movies. That's it. We need to disconnect our cable. I don't even like him. Really." Caitlyn found it hard to believe her own words, especially when the corners of her mouth curled up.

"You're so lying." Brittany slapped Caitlyn on the arm.

Caitlyn pushed her back. "You're coming, too."

The front door flew open, and a petite young woman rushed inside. She held her left hand up and waved it around. "Isn't this the most beautiful ring you've ever seen?" Hannah jumped up and down several times, her short, blond hair bouncing up and down with her. "Dave asked me to marry him, and I accepted."

"You did?" Brittany asked.

"He was so romantic, too. I never even expected it. He totally surprised me," Hannah sang out. "Look at this ring! It's gorgeous." She shoved her hand into Caitlyn's face.

"It's nice," Caitlyn said.

"We're getting married in December. I'm so excited," Hannah said.

"December, huh? Great month," Caitlyn said, not even attempting to hide her sarcasm.

"Congratulations," Brittany said. She gave her roommate a hug.

Caitlyn gave Hannah a hug and then walked down the hallway. Over her shoulder she said, "I have a test tomorrow. I'll see you in the morning."

"Better get your beauty rest for tomorrow night," Brittany called out to her.

Caitlyn shook her head and stepped into her room. She sat down on the bed and leaned over to grab something underneath it. She pulled out a white envelope and took out its contents. It read, "Mr. and Mrs. Robert Moore are pleased to announce the forthcoming marriage of their daughter, Caitlyn Marie, to Justin Oliver Haggerty, son of Mr. and Mrs. Petter Haggerty on the twenty-seventh day of December . . ." It fell from her hands.

seven

"I have a map to my home," said Professor Delbane. He adjusted his glasses and smoothed his barely-there gray hair. "We'll begin at 7:00 p.m. tomorrow evening. This is a get-together I sponsor for students who take this class. It gives us all a chance to get to know each other in a casual atmosphere, and it allows you to decide if education is the major you want to pursue." He walked over to the first row of chairs and handed out the papers. Caitlyn noticed his kind face.

This was her first real class in her major. She checked her watch. Only six more hours, thirteen minutes, and fifty eight seconds until her date with Travis. But who was counting? After all, she wasn't interested. Why didn't anyone believe her?

* * *

Caitlyn stared at her reflection. "My hair is lame. Maybe I should shave my head."

Brittany made a face at her in the mirror. "Seriously. You're so lucky to have naturally curly hair."

Caitlyn pulled her hair from one side to the other. "I still can't believe I let you streak my hair."

"I think you look hot."

"I'm not sure about this whole thing."

"Why?"

"I don't know." Caitlyn tugged at her hair some more. She put it behind her ears and then pulled it out. Then she grabbed a rubber band.

"Travis likes you."

"Even if that's remotely true, I'm not ready for this."

"You're just stressed because you've been out of the game for a little while." Brittany applied some eyeliner and then gazed at Caitlyn in the mirror. She said, "Actually, were you ever in the game?"

"Justin is the only one I've ever dated, and we all know how that turned out." Caitlyn made a ponytail and then let it down.

"I can't believe you never dated anyone else." Brittany smoothed on some lip gloss and puckered up her lips.

Caitlyn put her hair up in a half ponytail on top of her head. "How's this?"

"Awful." Brittany made a face.

Caitlyn batted her eyelashes at Brittany.

"My older brother always talks about how girls should have long hair and wear it down. He says all guys like long hair," Brittany said

Caitlyn let her hair fall down to right below her shoulders. She brushed it a few times. "Is this better?"

Brittany finger styled Caitlyn's waves. "There. Travis'll think you're irresistible."

Caitlyn gave Brittany a look. She picked up her toothbrush and swiped some toothpaste across it.

"It isn't an actual date for me, you know." Brittany sprayed some perfume on her wrist.

"Why not?" Caitlyn said with a mouthful of toothpaste bubbles.

"Travis is dragging his roommate along so he can go out with you," Brittany said.

"That's not true." Caitlyn cupped her hand under the faucet and caught some water. She slurped the water and rinsed out her mouth.

"Yes, it is. I'm sure it went something like this. 'Hey, how 'bout doing a mercy date and taking out Caitlyn's roommate? There's a movie in the deal.' Then Darren grunted his acceptance because of the movie." Brittany adjusted her shirt.

Caitlyn shook her head.

"It's okay, though, at least I get to see a movie and maybe he'll prove to be a new specimen."

"You're scamming on too many guys at once. One of these days, you'll actually have to settle for one, you know."

"Hmmm, what's the term for a woman with more than one husband?" Brittany smirked.

"Jail."

They were interrupted by the sound of knocking.

"I'm not ready." Caitlyn dashed to her bedroom. From her room, she could hear Brittany walk to the front door and open it.

"Hi, guys, come on in." Brittany's voice carried down the hall.

"This is my roommate Darren," Travis said. At the sound of his voice, Caitlyn's blood rushed through all of her veins at once.

Caitlyn looked in the mirror one more time and walked down the hall. Travis and Darren both stood.

"Hi, Travis," Caitlyn said.

"Hi. This is my roommate Darren."

"Hi, Darren." Caitlyn gave a short wave. She noticed why Brittany would be attracted to Darren. He was good-looking, but not anywhere near as attractive as Travis.

"Are we ready?" Travis said. They all walked out to the parking lot and stopped at a sleek black older-model Trans Am. Travis opened the door and let Darren and Brittany climb in the back. He helped seat Caitlyn in the front.

They pulled out of the parking lot. Caitlyn cleared her throat and said, "This isn't what I expected."

"Beg your pardon, Miss. I left the ol' pickup filled with manure at the ranch. I can exchange my car for it next time I go home if you'd feel more comfortable in that." Travis gave her a sideways glance.

He'd not only put her in her place, but his choice in vehicles intrigued her. Perhaps Travis was not the simple country boy that he first appeared.

On the way, they all exchanged small talk and admired the moderate temperature of the day. The theater was crowded, as usual, on Tuesday nights because tickets were offered at a reduced price. It was a popular hangout for financially-challenged college students.

Caitlyn, Travis, Darren, and Brittany all took their seats in the fourth row from the front. In the row ahead of them sat the Relief Society president in their ward and one of her counselors.

Caitlyn leaned up to speak to her friends. They visited for a few moments until the lights dimmed, and Caitlyn sat back against her velvet, padded seat. Immediately, she noticed that Travis had placed his arm around the chair and how subtly he then rested it on her shoulders. Instead of irritating her, it had the opposite effect.

Through the movie, she was surprised at how natural it felt to have his arm around her. She was even more surprised when she realized how much she liked it.

After the movie, Travis reached over and gently clasped her hand. She waved at a few other people she knew, and they walked up to the lobby.

Brittany glanced at their hands and gave Caitlyn a smile that said she knew exactly what was going on. Caitlyn gave her a quick nod.

"Should we head back to the apartments?" Travis asked.

Darren and Brittany looked at each other. Brittany shrugged her shoulders. "We think we'd like to walk."

"That's a long way," Travis said.

"Like miles," Caitlyn added. She was amazed at Brittany's ability to be interested in so many guys at once, yet make each one feel important.

"It'll give us a chance to talk," Darren said. He grabbed Brittany's hand.

"See you back at the apartment, Cait." Brittany's voice was light.

Travis opened the car door, and Caitlyn slid in. He shut the door, and she watched him walk around the front of the car. She didn't want to admit that for the first time since December, she felt rejuvenated.

Caitlyn opened the door to her apartment. She turned around, expecting Travis to say good night.

Instead he said, "Can I come in for a minute?"

"I'm sure I can find some gourmet water for you." She laughed.

Travis followed her into the living room and sat on the couch. He patted the cushion next to him and said, "Come sit down."

"Don't you want some of my secret-recipe water?" Caitlyn smiled extra wide.

"I'm fine, thanks." He patted the cushion again.

Caitlyn sat next to him. He leaned back. "Tell me about your family."

"Not much to say."

"You're from California, I know that."

Caitlyn nodded. "I have a younger sister named Lindsay. She's finishing her junior year. My dad is an accountant, and my mom is, well, my mom." She shrugged her shoulders. "And I've always lived in Santa Barbara."

"Do you surf?"

"A little. Mainly, I play tennis."

"Did you play in high school?"

"Yeah." Caitlyn adjusted her position on the couch

"Were you good?"

Caitlyn feigned shock. "Are you kidding? I was on fire."

"Sorry, I didn't realize who I was talking to." Travis held up his hands.

"You got that right," she said with attitude.

"Do you play tennis for BYU?"

"I wish. I came to BYU for other reasons."

"Like what?"

"Education, of course."

"Of course."

"I'm serious. BYU is a great school. I was so relieved when I was accepted my freshman year, although my dad wasn't too thrilled."

She leaned back against the couch.

"Why not?"

Caitlyn hesitated. She reached up and started twirling her hair. "He's not really supportive of BYU." Caitlyn felt a bit uncomfortable. She didn't want to tell Travis about her dad because she worried he might judge her by her dad.

"Is he a member?" Travis asked.

Caitlyn was startled by his direct question. She decided to give him a direct answer. "No, he's not."

"That must be hard." Sincerity laced his voice.

"Actually, I think it's made me stronger because I had to fight for my own testimony. It's not based on anyone else's, and it wasn't handed to me. I had to work hard for it, and now, I own it."

Travis peered into her eyes, and a warm feeling surrounded her. Travis reached over and briefly touched her hand. Electric pulses shot through her, and she was shocked to feel such a deep connection with someone she hardly knew.

"I'm glad you came to BYU."

Caitlyn cleared her throat and said, "You have a big family, right?"

"Yep. Mostly girls, though."

"Is that bad?"

"Only when it comes to bathroom time or lifting bales of hay."

"Are you saying girls aren't as strong as guys?" Caitlyn sat up straight.

"When it comes to throwing bales up on a hay wagon, I'd say that's true."

"Are you a male chauvinist?" Caitlyn placed her hands on her hips.

"I'll make you a deal. You can come over any time and try to load some bales and then ask me that question."

"It's a deal. I've never been to a ranch before."

Travis grinned. "This I gotta see."

Caitlyn slugged him in the arm. Somehow, he made her feel at ease and nervous at the same time. She hadn't felt anything like this since Justin. Actually, if she was brutally honest with herself, she'd never felt this way with Justin.

"I better get going. I have to be up early in the morning." He stood.

"Class?" She jumped to her feet.

"No, I'm milking cows."

"Here?"

"Down in Springville at a dairy."

"You actually squeeze milk out of cows?" Caitlyn scrunched up her nose.

"That's generally how it's done."

"I just buy it in a jug at the store."

"Someone has to get it out of the cow first. They don't drop milk jugs down from the sky." He smiled.

"I know that." She slugged him in the arm again. "Do you have class after that?"

"Right now, I'm working, trying to save some money to go to school and pay for my car. I milk in the morning and then work at Albertsons over on Center Street."

"Can't your parents pay for school?"

"Nope, we're poor cattle ranchers."

"I didn't mean . . ." Caitlyn felt her cheeks heat up.

"Don't worry about it, no offense taken."

Travis walked to the front door. "Are you busy tomorrow night?"

"No, I'm free." Caitlyn's voice cracked.

"Great, how about—"

Caitlyn cut him off, "Oh, sorry, I have a meeting at my teacher's house at 7:00. It's a get-to-know-you thing."

"Can I come along?"

"What?" Caitlyn was taken aback.

"To your thing?"

"I guess that'd be fine. You might be bored, though."

"I'll be over here about 6:30."

Caitlyn nodded.

"See you tomorrow night."

Caitlyn watched him walk down the stairs and out of sight.

She shut the door and leaned against it. What was happening? Did Travis actually like her or was he taking the role of FHE dad a little too far? And how did she feel about him?

She left the door and lay down on the couch. She closed her eyes for a moment when the door opened and Hannah burst in. Hannah stood at the door, waving good-bye to someone for almost a minute.

"I'm so excited," Hannah said as she shut the door and walked into the living room.

Caitlyn sat up. "Have you told your family about your engagement?"

"Huh?"

"Your mom and dad. Do they know you're engaged to Dave?"

"Not yet." Hannah bit her lip.

"Why not?"

Hannah sat down next to Caitlyn. "I need a little time."

"Why?"

Hannah gazed around the room. "They might not be as excited as I am."

Caitlyn nodded.

"Just because Dave isn't a member of the Church doesn't mean he's a bad person."

"Did I say that?"

"No, but you were thinking it, I could tell." Hannah's eyes filled with tears. "Dave's a good person. He'll get baptized some day, I know he will."

"Are you sure?"

"Yes." She wiped at her eyes.

"Why haven't you told your parents then?"

"I've been too caught up in everything, I guess."

"Or you know it's not the right decision."

Hannah turned to Caitlyn. "What makes you such an authority?"

"I've lived it all my life."

Hannah did a double take.

"That's right. My mom was super active in the Church. She

went to seminary and was even Laurel class president. She had quotes from the prophets hanging on her walls and wrote in her journal about temple marriage all the time. My dad transferred into her high school their senior year and before she knew it, she was in love with him."

"Is that bad?"

"He wasn't a member of the Church, and even though my mom had planned to only marry in the temple, when she met my dad, and they started dating, that was it."

"Oh."

"Of course, they were only friends at first. She was on the school council so she showed him around. They went to a few movies and then started spending more and more time together. By the end of their senior year, they were together all the time. My mom didn't think it was that big of a deal because they were still in high school. My grandparents begged her to wait and take time to think about it, but by that time she was so in love with my dad that nothing my grandparents said mattered."

"But, they're married in the temple now, right?"

"Nope."

"But, your dad's a member?"

"No again."

"He must be taking the missionary discussions."

"No, Hannah, he's not. He doesn't believe in the Church. He loves my mom and me and my sister, but, and this is the big thing, we aren't sealed together as a family. That bothers me."

Hannah looked down at her feet.

Caitlyn continued, "My dad's a great person, but he refuses to join the Church. I don't think he realizes how much that hurts my mom or me."

"I'm sure it'll be different with Dave." Hannah nodded.

"Really?"

"Sure. He'll join."

"My mom has been hoping that for over twenty years. She's often told me that she should've listened to my grandparents. She should've taken time to really think about what she was doing."

Caitlyn put her arm around her roommate.

"I don't think he's interested in the Church right now."

"Then wait."

"I don't think he will."

"What will happen when you have kids? What will they believe?" Caitlyn recalled her own confusion when she was young.

"That's so far into the future. Besides, it'll be different than it was for your parents. We'll get married and then go to the temple in a year or so. You'll see. It'll all work out."

"I hope you're right."

Hannah pasted on a smile, jumped up, and walked down the hall to her bedroom.

Caitlyn stepped into the kitchen and opened the refrigerator door. She stuck her head in and abruptly pulled it out. "We've got to clean this thing out before we're fined for toxic waste."

The door opened and Brittany jumped inside. "Hey, how was your date with Tra-vis?" Brittany accentuated each syllable of his name.

"He asked me out for tomorrow night." Caitlyn tried not to smile.

"Woo-hoo! You're on a roll. He's hot. You could get lost in those dark blue eyes."

"I hadn't noticed." Caitlyn said it with a solemn face. She smiled and said, "Looks like you had a good time with Darren."

"He's pretty hot, too. His blue eyes and long eyelashes really get to me." Brittany fanned herself with her hands.

"Even if it was a mercy date?" Caitlyn pushed Brittany's side.

"I take that back. I had fun, and I think he did, too. We ended up getting a ride back with one of his buddies that saw us walking. His friend is hot, too."

Caitlyn shook her head.

"And I heard Garrett is free now."

Caitlyn gave Brittany another push. "I can't keep up with you. Will you ever settle down?"

"Why choose only one guy when there's so many up here? It's like a giant salad bar."

"A what?"

"You can find any kind of guy you want and try out all sorts of different types to see what you like best." Brittany nodded.

Caitlyn rolled her eyes and said, "I can't believe you said that. I'm going to bed."

"See you in the morning." Brittany walked down the hall singing to herself.

eight

Alison adjusted the rearview mirror in her car. She checked her makeup and shook her long hair. Exhilaration enveloped her as she thought about her future with Travis. Today would mark a new beginning in their life together, she was sure of it. After all, they were cut from the same rural cloth, they understood each other, and they were meant to be together. She grabbed the picnic basket on the passenger seat.

Travis was stacking cans of green beans at the end of the aisle when Alison snuck up behind him, set the basket quietly on the ground, and placed her hands across his eyes. "Guess who?"

"Mom?"

"No, silly," Alison said in her sweetest voice. "It's me, of course." She removed her hands from his face.

"Alison? What are you doing here?"

"I thought you might enjoy a picnic." She smiled and picked up the basket.

"Here?"

"No, not in the store. In the park across the street. It's a beautiful day with plenty of sunshine. I've made my special barbecue chicken, some coleslaw, my homemade rolls you love so much, and chocolate chip cookies for dessert." She opened the top of the basket slightly.

"Sounds delicious." He glanced at his watch. "It's about time for my lunch break."

"I know." She gave Travis a look out of the corner of her eye. Didn't he realize she knew everything about him?

They crossed the street to Pioneer Park and found a picnic table under the shelter.

Alison reached into the basket and pulled out a tablecloth. She whipped it in the air and let it float down to settle on the table. She proceeded to set the table with china plates, silverware, and cut crystal glasses. "Only the best for you."

Travis sat across from Alison. "This is amazing. You're a great cook."

"I think it's important to know how to be a homemaker. I love to cook. Of course, you know that. You've known me forever," she said coyly.

"You're right. I remember being in Primary together."

"And junior high. Remember when we took home ec?"

"I forgot about that. We made quite a pizza." Travis laughed. He took a bite of coleslaw.

"And we can't forget our senior year in high school, or the prom. I still have our photo hanging up in my room. You looked so awesome in that black tux."

Travis filled his mouth with chicken.

"My mom says we looked like the bride and groom on top of a wedding cake. Isn't that sweet?"

"This chicken is superb, Alison. You really know how to get to a guy."

"Do I?" She leaned across the table.

Travis raised his arm and checked his watch. "My lunch break is almost up. I better get back to work."

"So soon?"

"I've got to earn some money if I ever want to go to BYU."

"But we haven't even had dessert yet."

"I'm sorry, Alison."

"That's okay. I'll come by your apartment after you get off work. We can eat the cookies, and I can pick up my photos.

Maybe we can even catch a movie?"

"Sounds fun, but I can't do it tonight."

"Oh. Well, you can take these home with you anyway." She handed him the plate of cookies covered in pink plastic wrap.

"I'm sure they'll be excellent. Thanks for bringing me lunch." Travis jogged across the grass grasping the plate of cookies.

Alison sat at the table and used her fork to play with the cole-slaw on her plate. She stabbed a piece of chicken. In a loud whisper, she said, "What am I going to do with you, Travis James Dixon? Why are you so dense? I practically throw myself at you, and you run off to work. Maybe I'm the one that needs to propose."

Alison packed up the lunch and headed to her car. On her drive back to her apartment, she noticed a bridal shop. She whirled her car around and parked behind the building.

"Hello. Can I help you find something?" a short older woman with a wide waist asked.

"Ah, yes. I'm looking for something flowing. And white, of course."

"I think I can find something for you. Why don't you have a seat, and I'll bring in some gowns."

Several minutes later, the sales lady brought several gowns and hung them up next to a room. She pulled the first one out and showed it to Alison. "This is a new design and uses the fabric on the bias. You can see how it flows at the bottom."

"It's beautiful."

"When are you getting married, dear?"

"We aren't totally engaged, yet. But it's only a matter of time. We've known each other forever, and we're a perfect match. I'm sure we'll get officially engaged soon, and I want to be prepared when it happens."

"Preparation is important, especially when it comes to a wedding. We also have lovely bridesmaid's dresses."

Alison picked up one of the other gowns and held it up to her. She peered into the mirror and said, "It's only a matter of time."

nine

Caitlyn was certain the arms on the clock were running counter-clockwise. Economics was torture enough without the added worry about the approaching date, if that's what she could call it, with Travis. Why did he want to come to some boring get-together for her class?

She glanced up at the clock and noticed only one minute had passed. Time was definitely stretching itself.

"Read chapter eight and answer all the review questions, including the essay questions. You can hand them in at the beginning of class tomorrow," said the short, stocky man with his familiar fiendish grin. He seemed to take pleasure in assigning immense amounts of homework.

Caitlyn left the building with her abnormally large textbook in hand, lugging her backpack across her shoulder. Mentally she tallied up at least five assignments that had to be completed before classes started tomorrow morning and this get-together at her professor's house would probably take a big chunk out of her evening. She headed over to the Harold B. Lee Library intent on finishing some of her homework.

Darren intercepted her in the foyer. "Hey, Caitlyn."

"Hi, Darren."

"What's up?" He smiled.

She held up her book. "Economics."

"Oh." Darren stood there in uncomfortable silence.

"Do you need something?"

He cleared his throat. "I was wondering."

"About?"

"Brittany." It seemed as if a heavy load had been lifted from him.

"Oh."

"Is she dating anyone in particular?" Darren's voice cracked.

"No, I wouldn't say that." Caitlyn shook her head.

"Do you think she'd go out with me again?"

"Sure. Brit goes out with every . . . I mean, she'd be happy to go out with you again." Caitlyn remembered the salad bar comparison and forced herself to smile at Darren.

"Thanks." Darren gave a little shrug and walked off.

Poor lovelorn guy. Would he be the lettuce, the bacon bits, or the bland salad dressing? One of these days, Brittany would have to settle down. It'd be interesting to see if Darren might be the one to tame her.

Caitlyn found an unoccupied table near the back of the fourth floor. It looked drab and dreary, especially since she could hear the soft, warm breeze calling her name. She wanted to spend time in the pool instead of in the library, but she was at BYU to get her education, not spend time lounging at the pool, as her dad often reminded her.

She turned to chapter eight in her economics book and began reading. She read the words but they didn't make any sense. "Why would anyone ever want to know this stuff?" she asked out loud. She forced herself to read on and on. Before she knew it, she opened her eyes and lifted her head. She wiped the drool from the side of her mouth and hoped no one had witnessed her studying by osmosis.

She gazed up at the clock. An hour and a half had passed since she'd started reading the chapter, and she hadn't finished any of her homework. She slammed the book closed and grabbed her backpack. She was done for the day because in a few hours Travis would be at her door.

She shook her head. What was she thinking? The memory of what happened with Justin still burned in her heart and she couldn't take a repeat performance. Besides, it wasn't in her plans to get involved with Travis or anyone else. Of course, all her planning about Justin didn't get her too far down the road of eternal bliss. So what did she know?

*   *   *

"Come on in, Travis," Brittany said loud enough for the neighbors to hear. Caitlyn's hand shook while she applied a bit of mascara, which she attributed to hunger or lack of sleep or something other than the date with Travis. She smoothed her black Capris and adjusted her hot pink shirt.

She walked slowly down the hall, trying to calm her racing heartbeat. The last thing she wanted was for Travis to think he made her nervous. When she spotted Travis, though, her heartbeat sped up so much she thought it might explode. "Hi, Travis." She hoped her voice didn't betray her.

"You look nice," Travis said in a sincere tone.

"Thanks." Her heartbeat thumped in her ears.

"Shall we make like a tree and leave?" Travis grinned.

Caitlyn shook her head. "I haven't heard that since third grade."

*   *   *

On the way over to her professor's house, Caitlyn and Travis discussed music. She discovered he preferred twangy country music while she only listened to pop.

"There it is, 1632." Caitlyn pointed to a gray colonial style house with black trim.

"Seems to be quite a few people here. I'll have to park down the street a bit."

"It's my entire class and their, uh, well, whoever came with them." Caitlyn waved her hand. She hoped the get-together would end quickly and uneventfully.

Travis parked his car around the corner from the professor's house. He jumped out, opened the door for Caitlyn, and extended his hand. She reached out and, sure enough, it was the same electric heat she'd felt the night before. Something was definitely happening, and she was finding it more and more difficult to stop it or to deny it.

The white front door opened, and her professor said, "Welcome. Come in and find a seat." He led them into a large room with traditional dark wood furniture and some folding chairs. They found two chairs by the red brick fireplace.

"I think everyone is here, now. I'm glad you could all make it. This get-together seems to make us all feel more relaxed. I'd like everyone to take a few moments to introduce themselves." The professor found a seat next to an obviously newly-married couple.

"My name is Lance Jackson, and I'm from Albuquerque, New Mexico," said a guy with bright red hair and freckles. "My dad's a high school principal. He thinks I should be a teacher. I think I like kids, I don't have any, but they seem to be okay, I guess." He sat down abruptly and Caitlyn met eyes with Travis.

After several other students introduced themselves, a small Hispanic girl with short black hair and large brown eyes stood. In a slight accent she said, "My name is Rosa Jones. I'm from Mexico. This is my husband, Richard. I met him here at BYU last year. He was the father of our family home evening group and I was the mother." She giggled. Her husband reached up and grabbed her hand.

Suddenly, the room shrunk around Caitlyn and her ears warmed. What were the odds of someone sharing a story like that when she and Travis were also serving as . . . embarrassment whacked her in the head.

Her classmate continued, "We've been married for a few months now. I've always loved education, and I'm so happy to be here." She sat down and her husband snuggled close to her.

Caitlyn's face burned, and her heart felt like it was beating a thousand times a minute. She didn't dare look at Travis, but she could feel him smirking. Who wanted to know that she met her husband in their FHE group? Her teacher didn't ask them to give that much information. Now Travis would think that she somehow manipulated him into coming because she had marriage on her mind. Where was the nearest trash can so she could throw up?

Finally, it was Caitlyn's turn. "My name is Caitlyn Moore, and I'm from California. I'm a sophomore, and this is my first class in this major."

"Is this your husband?" her teacher asked while motioning to Travis.

Caitlyn felt her tongue swell to three times its size. "Uh . . . no. This is Travis Dixon."

"Hi, nice to meet you." Travis stuck out his hand and shook Professor Delbane's hand.

"What's your major, Travis?"

"I'm working right now, sir, hoping to save some money for next fall." Travis gave a nod.

"Welcome to our class for the evening." The professor went on to talk about education issues. After an hour, he concluded his remarks.

"My wife has made some refreshments. Please, feel free to visit among yourselves and ask me any questions you might have. Thank you for coming tonight."

Caitlyn let out a breath and leaned over to Travis. "I'm sorry this took so long. It must have bored you to death."

"No way. I'm very interested in education. I plan to have at least twelve kids."

Caitlyn coughed.

"Twelve kids or maybe even a baker's dozen."

Caitlyn stared at him. Was he kidding?

"The scriptures say, 'He who hath his quiver full . . .' "

Caitlyn leaned back and blinked her eyes several times. She glanced over at Travis who was wearing a grin that covered his entire face. "Gotcha."

Caitlyn laughed, but she wasn't convinced he didn't mean what he said.

Travis stood. "I'll get us some refreshments." Caitlyn watched him walk over to the table. He was not at all like Justin. They couldn't be more opposite in their looks or their personalities. Travis was cheerful and he liked to joke around. Most of the time he was funny, or at least he thought so.

"I hope you like brownies." Travis handed her a small plate.

Caitlyn's eyes grew big. "Did you leave anything for anyone else?"

"I wanted to give you a variety of choices."

Caitlyn looked around and said, "Where's your plate?"

"Didn't get one. I told everyone at the table you had quite an appetite, and we'd already had dinner."

"No, you didn't!"

"Yep. I did." He clicked his tongue.

"I have to go to class with these people. They're going to think I have some eating disorder."

"Yeah, that one where you eat everything in sight." Travis spread his arms out.

"What else did you say?"

"Hmmm." Travis crossed his arms in front of his chest.

"I give up." Caitlyn shrugged.

"Might as well." Travis reached over and grabbed a chocolate chip cookie from her plate.

They finished up their refreshments, thanked her teacher, and walked outside. Travis leaned against the car. "Beautiful night tonight." Travis gazed upward. "You can't see as many stars here, though. When you look up at the sky on a clear night at home, the stars look like little shards of glass against the black sky."

Caitlyn watched him watch the stars. She felt compelled to wrap her arms around him, but she resisted. Her attraction to him was growing, despite her fear of another broken heart.

"I've spent many a night out under the stars. Grandpa liked to take me with him, even when I was pretty young, to help with the cows."

Caitlyn leaned against the car too, and looked heavenward.

Travis scooted closer to her and her breath caught in her throat.

"I used to have a horse. His name was John and he was huge. When we were out herding and it'd start raining, I'd sleep under him. He'd stand in one place all night. He was a great horse." Travis nodded.

He glanced at his watch under the moonlight. "It's getting late, we better get back." He opened the car door for Caitlyn.

"Can we stop by the lockers in the Wilkinson Center? I forgot to bring something home today," Caitlyn said.

*   *   *

Travis pulled up in front of the Wilkinson Center.

"It'll only take me a minute. I'll be right back." Caitlyn hopped out of the car and darted into the building. She was back in a flash.

She placed a box on her lap but said nothing.

"What's in there?" Travis asked as they drove away from the Wilkinson Center.

"It's a secret." She didn't crack a smile.

"Maybe I'll have to force it out of you then." Travis flexed his right arm.

"I'd like to see you try. I know karate." Caitlyn muttered a few oriental-sounding words.

"Okay, okay, I know when I'm out-powered." He laughed and placed his hand on Caitlyn's. She welcomed the warmth.

"It's something for Friday. I'm volunteering a little time. No big deal." She shrugged.

"I was thinking we could get together tomorrow night. Maybe play a game of miniature golf?" Travis said.

"I don't know. I'm a pretty amazing miniature golfer. I've won awards, and I've even been inducted into the miniature golfing hall of fame. Maybe you've read about me?" She blew on her fingers and then rubbed them on her chest.

Now, it was Travis who did a double take. "I can see I've met my match."

"I don't know what you mean." Caitlyn played innocent.

"Don't worry. I'm up to the challenge of matching wits." Travis raised his eyebrows.

Caitlyn smiled. Travis was not only attractive, he was interesting, and their conversation was easy and lively.

"Tomorrow night?" Travis said as he parked the car.

"I'll have to check my planner." Caitlyn made a serious face.

"Say yes." Travis accentuated a nodding motion.

"Okay . . . I guess . . . yes."

They exited the car and walked over to Caitlyn's apartment door. She leaned against the wall. "Thanks for taking me tonight."

"You're most welcome." Travis bowed.

Caitlyn paused for a moment. Would he kiss her? If he did, would she kiss him back? Her stomach contracted while she considered the implications of her thoughts.

"I'll be here about 7:00 tomorrow night."

"See you then." She waited.

Travis leaned in close enough that she could smell his cologne. He opened the door for her. She stepped into the apartment. "Do you want to come in?" She hoped he wouldn't detect the anxiety in her voice.

"I better call it a night. I'll see you tomorrow, though. Good night."

Disappointment that he hadn't kissed her swelled up in her chest. She'd only known Travis a few days. How could she want to kiss him? She slapped herself on her cheek. "Snap out of it. Remember Justin."

ten

Caitlyn surveyed the lunch crowd in the Cougareat hoping to spot Brittany. She noticed a wave and walked toward a table in the back of the food court.

"I picked up my costume for Special Olympics last night and I think I'm ready for it tomorrow."

"I can't believe you're going to dress up in a clown suit all day." Brittany shrugged. "Maybe you'll see some hot guys while you're there."

Caitlyn shot her roommate a look. "I'm not volunteering at Special Olympics to meet guys. I'm doing it to help with the athletes. Not everyone is as obsessed with guys as you are."

Brittany took a big bite of her bean burrito.

"You should come to Special Olympics. Last year when I volunteered it was awesome. You should volunteer."

"Me? Volunteer? That's something to think about, I guess." Brittany eyed the crowd. "Oh, don't look now, but there's Hannah and Dave."

Caitlyn turned her head to catch a glimpse of her absentee roommate.

"Good thing you're not obvious," Brittany said.

"I hope she doesn't marry him. He can't take her to the temple. And even I, the official poster girl for temple wedding dumpees, know there's no other place to get married."

"Speaking of that, how was your date with Travis last night?" Brittany took another bite of her burrito.

"It wasn't a date, exactly."

In a high-pitched voice Brittany said, "I think you're starting to fall for the hick farmer."

"Am not."

"Are too."

"I've seen another side to him, though. I'm not saying I like him or anything, but maybe he's not as bossy or annoying as I thought on Sunday."

"You're falling hard." Brittany finished eating her burrito.

"No way. I don't plan to do that for a very long time, if ever."

"But you have to admit, there's definite chemistry between the two of you." Brittany slurped her soda.

"Maybe, but—"

Brittany laid her head back. "Not the Justin thing."

"I'm so over Justin. It's just that—"

"You're a chicken." Brittany clucked a few times.

Caitlyn sighed. "Justin demolished me. I'm not ready for that again."

"You have to take a chance someday, or you'll end up sitting in a rocking chair, knitting, and talking to yourself."

"I don't want to get hurt again." Caitlyn emphasized her words.

"Travis isn't Justin. You need to give him a chance." Brittany took a bite of her soft taco.

"I'm not even sure he's interested in me."

"What do you need? A chorus of angels? He's asked you out the last two nights in a row."

"I don't even know him that well. It's only been a few days." Caitlyn pulled a pepperoni from her pizza.

"How well do you need to know him?" Brittany yanked a pepperoni from Caitlyn's pizza and popped it in her mouth.

"Well enough to know he won't hurt me."

"Cut that Justin weight from around your neck and move on.

Travis is gorgeous. He seems like a nice guy, and he likes you." Brittany tapped Caitlyn on the hand.

"We're going miniature golfing tonight."

Brittany laughed.

"What? I'm not that bad at mini golf." Caitlyn sat up.

"You're pretty bad."

They continued chatting until Brittany left for her 1:00 class. Caitlyn took her time with the rest of her lunch and then walked slowly back to her apartment.

eleven

"You look awesome. Stop stressing out," Brittany said.

"I'm not stressed." Caitlyn brushed her hair, again.

"Why have you changed your outfit five times? Or is it six?"

"I wanted to find the most comfortable clothes for golfing so I can play a good game. That's all." Caitlyn tugged at her shirt.

"Yeah, right." Brittany munched on a chocolate-covered granola bar.

"Okay, I admit it. I want to look good for Travis. Are you happy?"

"Yep."

"You're right. I can't explain it, but I think I'm falling for him. All I could think about today was this date. It sounds ridiculous since I've only known him a few days," Caitlyn took a deep breath, "but I think I'm ready to take a chance again."

"Relax. It'll go well, trust me. Have I ever headed you in the wrong direction?"

"Today?"

Brittany slugged her in the arm. "I'm glad you've finally admitted you have feelings for him and, better yet, you're willing to give him a chance. You'll have fun tonight, I'm sure of it."

"I wonder . . ."

"What?"

Caitlyn covered her face.

"What?" Brittany said it louder.

Caitlyn still said nothing.

"If he'll kiss you?" Brittany jumped up and down. "That's it, isn't it?"

Caitlyn removed her hands slightly from her face.

"You want him to kiss you?"

"I didn't say that. I'm not sure I'm ready."

"Even thinking about it shows hope for you." Brittany slapped Caitlyn on the back a few times.

"But, what if—"

Brittany raised her hand. "Don't even say it. Travis is not Justin."

"I know, but—"

Brittany covered Caitlyn's mouth. "No buts. Go out tonight. Have fun. Don't even think about Justin. His name is banished from this apartment forever." She removed her hand.

"I haven't been this excited for a long time."

"I hate to break this up, but I've got to finish a paper. I want details, though, as soon as you get home. Every juicy detail—leave nothing out. Promise?"

Caitlyn tried not to smile, but it crept across her face until it smothered every inch. "Promise."

6:55 p.m. Travis would be knocking on the door any minute. Caitlyn's heart thudded so hard she wondered if it might burst out of her chest. She sipped some water and tried to calm her nerves. What if he did kiss her? What would that mean? She wiped her moist palms on her faded jeans.

7:10 p.m. It wasn't like Travis to be late. She paced the hallway and checked her makeup and hair in the bathroom mirror. She brushed her hair several times and attempted to pat the waves a bit flatter. She noticed the electric yellow streaks were beginning to grow out.

Ten more minutes passed. He'd never been this late, at least not in the whole four days she'd known him. She gulped another glass of water. She adjusted the collar of her lime-colored shirt and put

73

on another coat of lip gloss. Her nerves continued to gnaw at her stomach.

Brittany emerged from her bedroom. "What time was he supposed to be here?" She reached into the cabinet and pulled out a package of chocolate covered cookies. "I need brain food for this paper."

"7:00, I think. Maybe I heard him wrong."

"Want one?" Brittany handed her a cookie. "Let's turn on the TV and see what's on. It'll make the time go by faster. Besides I need a break."

"You only started your paper a half hour ago."

"Yeah, but in the time warp continuum it's really been several hours." Brittany snatched the remote and turned on the TV. They both sat on the couch.

"You surf through channels like a guy," Caitlyn said.

"Sorry. What do you want to watch?"

"Actually, it doesn't matter." Caitlyn bit at her fingernail.

They continued to scan channels, making only momentary stops. Brittany glanced over at the clock on the wall. She said, "8:00. I wonder where he is."

Caitlyn rubbed her temples. Disappointment, anger, and sadness wrapped around her. When she least expected it, she'd been annihilated. Again.

"Maybe there was a problem or something."

"Yeah, I'd say there was a problem." Caitlyn rolled her eyes. "I should never have trusted him or listened to you."

"Why? Where do you think he is?"

"Isn't it obvious?" Caitlyn folded her arms across her chest.

"No."

"How could I have been such an idiot, again?" Caitlyn sighed. "When will I learn?"

"You've lost me."

"He's with another girl while I'm sitting here waiting. What a jerk."

"That's a jump, isn't it? Give the guy a break," Brittany said.

"Justin, Travis, they're all the same." Caitlyn shook her hands in the air. "I should've known better, that's all. I deserve this. I knew this'd happen."

"Cait, you're way overreacting. There might be a good explanation. Maybe he'll call."

"I'm done with Travis." Caitlyn stood up and stomped off down the hall. She slammed her bedroom door bchind her.

She threw herself on her bed. How could she have been so blind? Just when she thought she could open her heart again—bam!

All of the anguish she'd experienced in front of the temple billowed up inside, and she felt nauseated. She placed the crook of her elbow across her face and berated herself for being such a fool until she finally fell asleep.

twelve

Caitlyn rolled over, slapped off the radio alarm, and pulled the pillow over her head. After several minutes, she sat up. She caught a glimpse of herself in the mirror across the room. Even from this distance she could see her mascara stained cheeks and swollen eyes. But she didn't have time to feel sorry for herself. It was almost 7:30 and she needed to be down at the field across from Helaman Halls for Special Olympics by 8:15.

She dragged herself out of bed and wandered into the bathroom. She splashed cold water on her face and attempted to remove last night's makeup. A thought of Travis tried to creep into her mind, but she pushed it aside. No, she pummeled it aside.

She grabbed the box she'd brought home and opened it. She reached in and grabbed a colorful mix of material. She held it up—a clown suit. A wig lay in the box, too. "Cheer up. The kids at Special Olympics don't want a depressed clown hugging them at the finish line," she said to herself while she patted her cheeks.

Caitlyn put on the outfit and the rainbow wig. Next, she drew lipstick circles on her cheeks and dabbed it on the end of her nose. She took an eye-liner pencil and made long eyelashes on her cheeks and colored in triangle eyebrows. The makeup hid her puffy eyes.

She adjusted the wig and tied a neon green belt around her trim waist when her cell phone rang. She trudged into the kitchen and answered, "Hello."

"Caitlyn?" She recognized the voice.

"Yep." Brave of him to call so soon after standing her up.

"This is Travis."

"Uh-huh." What excuse would he give her?

"About last night."

"Yeah?" She kept her voice cool.

"Our date."

"Did we have a date last night? Oh, no, did I forget or did I have something better to do?" Her anger mounted

"If you'll give me a chance, I'll explain." He sounded sincere.

"Go ahead, I guess." She removed the phone momentarily and then switched it to the other ear.

He cleared his throat and she braced for the excuse. She hoped at least it'd be an original one. "I really wanted to see you last night."

"Uh-huh."

"But I had a little problem."

A little problem, huh? What was her name?

"Caitlyn?"

"I'm still here." *Barely.*

"I had a car accident."

She jerked her head back. "A what?"

"On the freeway."

She stood there, her mouth hanging open.

"Kind of messed up my leg."

Caitlyn shook her head. She blinked several times and said, "Are you okay?"

"Yeah. I'm still in the hospital. I was here last night, that's why I didn't make our date."

"Don't worry about that. I knew something must've come up," Caitlyn fibbed. She sat on a chair by the kitchen table. "Can I do something?" She clenched her jaw and closed her eyes. She wanted to slap herself, hard.

"I'd enjoy a visit." She could hear the cheerfulness in his voice.

"I've got a commitment until 4:00, but I'll come by after that."

"Sounds good. I really am sorry about last night."

"I'm sorry you're in the hospital." She clutched her chest.

"I'll see you later, then?"

"Yes."

Caitlyn closed her phone. She felt like the gum on the bottom of someone's shoe. She was pretty harsh in her judgment of Travis last night and jumped to conclusions that weren't even remotely true. Now, he was in the hospital, and she was an idiot.

*　　*　　*

Soft sunshine fell on her shoulders and back as she made her way across the parking lot and over to the field. Thick green grass spanned out in front of her and a slight breeze fanned her face. Crowds of people thronged the bleachers.

Volunteers and participants covered the fields. Caitlyn was one of a few clowns whose job description included plenty of hugs for each athlete at the finish line.

*　　*　　*

"Hey, Cait."

Caitlyn turned. "Brit, you made it."

"I thought I'd come check it out. Do you get a break?"

Caitlyn glanced at her watch. "Perfect timing. Let's grab a soda."

They located a shady spot under a tree by the fence. "How's things?" Brittany said in a light tone.

"Fine."

"I thought you'd still be mad about last night." Brittany opened her can of soda.

"You mean when Travis ditched me?" Caitlyn opened her can and the contents sprayed her hand. She shook her hand and then wiped it on the grass.

"You were so not happy when you went to bed."

Caitlyn tried to keep her face emotionless. "He called."

Brittany's eyes grew large. "What did he say?"

"He was in an accident."

"A what?"

"A car accident."

"Is he okay?"

"He's still in the hospital."

"And you're going to see him, of course."

"Hmmm." Caitlyn sipped her soda.

"Cait!"

Caitlyn pushed Brittany's arm. "Yes. I told him I'd come by later. I'll be done here about 4:00 and I'll go back to the apartment so I can shower and change."

"Why?" Brittany chugged some more soda and then let out an enormous burp.

Caitlyn shook her head. "Because, in case you haven't noticed, I'm dressed as a clown with a rainbow wig."

"You should go see him like this."

"No way."

"Where's your sense of adventure? You look awesome." Brittany patted Caitlyn's wig.

"I'd be way too embarrassed. I don't have a problem being a clown here, but at the hospital, in front of Travis? I don't think so."

"It'd be a visit he'd never forget."

Caitlyn leaned her head back. Brittany had a point. Travis would definitely remember her visiting him in a clown suit. Maybe it was worth considering.

Caitlyn adjusted her wig. "I'll think about it. I better get back, though."

"I'll see you later, and you can fill me in on your hospital visit." Brittany giggled.

thirteen

Alison stopped at the bathroom in the hospital lobby. She brushed her hair, applied some blush, and dabbed a bit of perfume on her wrist and behind her ear. She wanted to look her best for Travis to help cheer him up.

She caught the next elevator and watched each floor light up until the doors opened. She hurried down the corridor to the last room on the left.

"Travis," she said while she entered the room, "Tanya just called to tell me you were here." She rushed to the side of his bed.

"Alison. I'm sorry, I didn't get chance to call you yet."

"Don't even worry about that. What happened?" She caressed his arm.

"I was driving on the freeway and before I knew it, I was wearing a flat bed truck as a hood ornament."

"Still joking at a time like this. I've been trembling ever since I found out. I don't know what I'd do if . . ." She buried her head in his neck. "Oh, I'm sorry, did I hurt you?"

"No, it's mainly my leg. Although, I think I'll have some pretty cool scars from the glass in my arm. Look." He lifted his arm.

"Travis Dixon, I can't leave you for a minute. I'll have to give you lots of tender loving care to help you recuperate."

"I think I may need an operation on my leg."

Alison examined the damage. "Looks like a compound fracture. They'll have to wait until the swelling goes down before they can operate. You may need screws."

"You sound like one of the doctors."

"I wouldn't mind being your personal doctor." She winked at him.

The door opened and Tanya stepped through. "Alison."

"Tanya." They embraced for several moments. "I'm so glad you called me," Alison said.

"I'm surprised Travis didn't call you first." Tanya gave him a look, and he shrugged. "I'm glad you're here to help my little brother."

"You may have been born a few minutes ahead of me, but I'm not your little brother."

"When you're all healed up, you can prove that. But for now, you need rest."

"And I'm here to help," Alison said. She and Tanya gave each other a knowing smile. They hugged each other again. Travis waved his hand. "I hate to break up this happy reunion in my hospital room, but where's Mom?"

"She's back at the hotel. She wanted to take a nap. I think she's exhausted from everything. I told her I'd pick her up in a while so she can come see you. Dad said he'd try to drive up tomorrow or Sunday."

An older, skinny woman entered the room. "Mr. Dixon needs his rest. We'll be serving lunch soon."

"Please, call me Travis." He smiled at the nurse.

She nodded.

"Come on, Alison, let's go to lunch. We'll come back later." Tanya grabbed Alison's arm.

"But—" Alison tried to protest.

"I'm in great hands, right?" He glanced at the nurse.

Tanya placed her arm through Alison's, and they left the room.

*   *   *

"You aren't eating," Tanya said.

"I'm worried, that's all." Alison sat back.

"Travis will be fine. His leg is pretty messed up, but the doctor thinks he'll be up and around in no time. You know Travis."

"I'm worried about that, of course, but I'm also worried about us."

"Us?" Tanya held her hand out in front of her.

"Not you and me." Alison let out an exasperated breath. "The us that includes Travis and me."

"Haven't you been dating?"

"We were going out until a few weeks ago. Right about when he moved into his new apartment. After a week of not seeing him, I finally called and invited him to dinner on Sunday night."

"How did that go?" Tanya twisted her thick, dark hair and clipped it to the back of her head.

"He enjoyed the food, but he wasn't taking any of my hints. He can be so dense sometimes." Alison tapped her fingernails on the table.

"Did he say why he hadn't called?"

"He's been busy. I know he's working two jobs, but we need time together." She picked up her fork and pushed her salad around the plate.

"I'm sure it'll work out. You and Travis are made for each other. Haven't I said that since we were Beehives? I'm sure you'll work things out."

Alison leaned in and said, "I stopped by a bridal shop."

"You did?"

"The gowns were gorgeous. I made a down payment on one of them."

Tanya gasped. "Really?"

"And on a long veil with pearls around the edge." The thought of marrying Travis made her body tingle.

"I can't wait until you're my sister-in-law. We'll be sisters like we've always planned." Tanya clapped her hands.

"As long as Travis cooperates." Alison felt her frustration rise.

"Don't worry about that. He's always loved you, even though he may not realize it yet."

"We should come up with a solid plan."

"You're right." Tanya sipped her water.

Alison smiled. "He'll never know what hit him."

"It'll be like when we used to have Barbie be you and that Ken with real hair be Travis, and they'd get married and live happily ever after."

"Yeah, happily ever after . . ."

fourteen

Caitlyn jogged toward the front doors of the hospital. She saw her reflection in the glass and stopped. She reeled around and darted back toward her car. She leaned against the car for a few moments while she inhaled and exhaled slowly, trying to convince herself to unglue her feet from the pavement.

In her right hand she held an oatmeal-colored teddy bear she'd picked up on her way over to the hospital. She lifted the bear, peered into its smooth black eyes, and said, "I guess I not only look like a clown, but I'm acting like one, too. This is ridiculous, don't you think?"

She helped the bear nod its head.

"I'm going to go into that hospital and visit Travis. After all, he is the dad of my FHE group. I should go see him and make sure he's doing okay. No big deal, right?" She looked at the bear. "This doesn't mean anything. I'm dressed like this to cheer him up and, thankfully, he's the only one I know that will see me like this." She gazed at the bear. "Stop looking at me like that." She bopped the bear on its head and shoved it under her arm.

She waited at the elevator, chewing on her thumbnail. The doors opened and she stepped inside. The doors began to close when she heard a voice.

"Please, hold the elevator." It was a woman that appeared to be in her early-fifties with short brown hair and glasses.

She was followed by a much younger woman with darker hair that was secured by a large clip. The younger woman seemed familiar. Obviously, from their chattering, the older woman was the mother. They all rode up to the fourth floor.

The doors opened and Caitlyn exited. So did the two women. Caitlyn stopped at the nurses' station and waited for a few minutes to double check on Travis's room number. She didn't want to appear as a clown in just anyone's room.

Caitlyn's feet felt like hardened cement while she walked down the ever-growing corridor to the last room on the left. She finally arrived at the doorway and took a deep breath before she poked her head in.

"Hi, Travis."

"Caitlyn?" His grin enveloped his face. "Come in." He motioned with his hand.

She stepped into the room and embarrassment washed over her as she noticed the same two women from the elevator standing in the opposite corner of the room.

Travis pointed to the women and said, "Caitlyn, this is my mom and my sister, Tanya."

"Hello," Caitlyn said in a small voice. She pulled at her wig.

"Nice to meet you," his mother said with a warm smile.

"Caitlyn is the mom of my family home evening group." Travis winked.

Tanya eyed Caitlyn up and down.

"I wanted to come by and check on you before we get something to eat," his mom said.

"How about bringing me back some decent food?" Travis pleaded.

"You certainly love a good home-cooked meal," Tanya said with an edge Caitlyn didn't understand.

"I don't know about sneaking in food, Travis. Better eat what they serve you," his mom said.

"Come on, Mom, nothing big, just edible," Travis said.

"You must be feeling a bit better. I'll see what I can do." She leaned over and gave him a kiss on the forehead. "You scared me to death." She shook her finger at him. "Don't you ever do that again."

"I'll try not to, Mom." He nodded.

She turned to Caitlyn. "I like your outfit."

Caitlyn hoped her makeup covered her flushed face.

"See ya, Trav," Tanya said. She gave Caitlyn a peculiar look and turned around without saying a word. They left the room, and Caitlyn felt like she'd interrupted a private family reunion.

"I think I came at a bad time."

"Not at all. Sit your little clown self down."

"I'm sure you're wondering why I'm dressed like this." She gave a pose.

"Nope. I think I have that figured out."

"You do?"

"Is that for me?" Travis pointed at the teddy bear in Caitlyn's arms.

"Uh, yeah. I brought it to keep you company." She cleared her throat. "To remind you of our FHE group, of course."

"Of course. Let's put it over there so I can see it. Thanks."

Caitlyn rested the fluffy bear on the shelf over the sink. The bear seemed to have a smile on its face. She stepped over to the bed and said, "So, you broke your leg?" She glanced toward the bottom of the bed and noticed his right leg up on a pillow. Closer inspection showed an open wound with no dressing. Suddenly, a cold sweat erupted over her body, and she saw polka dots in front of her eyes. She found a chair next to the bed.

"It's a compound fracture. A pretty nasty one." He almost sounded proud.

"I can see that." She turned her head and covered her mouth.

"Are you feeling okay?" Travis asked.

"I'm fine." She coughed a couple of times. "How did the accident happen?"

"I was driving on the freeway when a guy in a flat bed truck pulled right in front of me and slammed on his brakes. I wanted to get out of the way, but it happened so fast, and there was a car next to me. I slammed on my brakes and then hit him, hard. I don't know what he was thinking."

Caitlyn shook her head. "Then what happened?"

"I forced myself to remain conscious. I figured if I stayed awake I wouldn't die. It seemed like hours before the ambulance got there. The EMT asked me all sorts of lame questions. I finally told him to stop asking me stuff and get me out of the stinkin' car. When I looked down at my right leg, I realized that my foot was on backwards."

"What?" Her eyes widened.

"When I hit the truck, the engine of my car landed on my leg, broke it, and somehow, my foot got turned around and lodged under the seat." Travis used his hands to describe it.

The walls started to dance and the floor began to wave.

"Are you sure you're okay?"

"Fine."

"You don't look too good."

"Thanks a lot. I spend all this time putting on my best makeup, and you tell me I don't look very good." The skin at the base of her neck felt clammy.

"No, I mean you look like you're going to pass out."

"I'm fine, really." She took a deep breath and slowly exhaled. "Go on with your story." The embarrassment of meeting his mom while dressed as a clown was still fresh in her mind, and she certainly didn't want to add to it. She willed herself to not faint.

"That's about it. They finally got me, and my leg, out. I still have glass in my forehead and arm from the windshield, and I hit my chin on the steering wheel, but my leg is the main problem. I'll be scheduled for surgery as soon as the swelling goes down." He pointed at his leg.

"How long will you be in here?" Caitlyn lowered her head and closed her eyes, concentrating on not thinking about his accident or his leg.

"Four or five days. Maybe a week."

After a few moments of silence Caitlyn said, "What can I do to help?" She started to feel better so she raised her head and peered at

Travis. The same strong attraction seized her.

"Seeing you in your clown suit has helped." Travis said with a big smile. "I guess you'll have to take charge of the FHE group."

"No problem. Can I get you anything now?" She pointed to a paper cup on the table. "Remember, I can make an amazing cup of water."

"Maybe you can stay for a while?"

*   *   *

Back at her apartment, Caitlyn took out some makeup remover and applied it to her face. Most of the makeup came off, although a slight red discoloration to her cheeks and the end of her nose remained.

"What happened at the hospital?" Brittany asked while she leaned against the wall next to the bathroom.

"It was a little weird." Caitlyn rubbed her cheeks with a tissue. "I rode in the elevator with a girl that seemed really familiar. Ended up being Travis's twin sister, Tanya."

"I don't get it. Why was it weird for her to be there?"

"It was how she acted. First, it seemed like she was surprised. Then it was like she wanted to get rid of me or something. She glared at me like this." Caitlyn narrowed her eyes as she imitated Tanya.

"Why would she do that?"

Caitlyn shrugged. "No idea."

fifteen

Caitlyn awoke to the smell of burnt toast. Saturday. No school. She rolled out of bed and plopped herself on the floor. She volleyed around the idea of visiting Travis again. What would he think? Would Tanya be there and act all weird?

Her door flung open. "How about laying around the pool, working on our tans, and checking out the guys?"

"Do you ever knock?"

Brittany shut the door and knocked on the back side of it. "How about laying around the pool, working on our tans, and checking out the guys?"

Caitlyn sighed.

"So?" Brittany hopped on Caitlyn's bed.

"I'm not sure."

"Are you going to hang out at the hospital?"

"I didn't say that." Caitlyn held up her hands.

"Why don't you go visit him and then we can go to the pool? It's a great day for lounging poolside."

"I'll make you a deal; I'll go to the pool if you come with me to the hospital." Caitlyn stuck out her hand.

Brittany shook Caitlyn's hand. "Deal."

The radio blasted while they drove across town to the hospital. Caitlyn rolled down the window and let the warm spring air rush through her hair. They bobbed their heads to the beat of the music. Caitlyn felt relieved to have Brittany accompany her to the hospital.

In the elevator, Brittany started dancing to the music. Caitlyn shook her head but then decided to join her. A little silliness never hurt anyone.

They walked down the corridor to Travis's room, and when they reached it, Brittany jumped inside the doorway. "Howdy, Travis." She waved her right arm.

"Brittany." His voice registered his surprise.

"Hey, Travis," Caitlyn said as she walked in behind her roommate.

"Hi. What brings you two out this morning? Are the Saturday morning cartoons over already?" He looked at his bare wrist.

"Thought we'd come over here to see what you're having for breakfast since Cait burned the toast this morning," Brittany said. She sat on the chair next to the bed and smiled at Caitlyn.

Travis whispered in a loud voice, "It's a little-known secret that the hospital chef trained in Paris."

"Apparently." Brittany poked at the food on the plate in front of Travis.

"How are you feeling today?" Caitlyn said.

"Okay, I think. I'm on so many pain killers, I'm not even sure of my name," Travis said with a laugh.

"Has your surgery been scheduled yet?" Caitlyn leaned against the wall.

"Probably Monday. The doctor thinks the swelling will be down by then and he can put me back together. He's planning to put some screws in my ankle and a plate in my leg. If I ever have to fly anywhere, I'll set off all the airport security alarms."

Brittany stood and walked to the end of the bed. She investigated his leg. "Whoa, that's messed up. At least you gave it your full effort and didn't do some lame break."

"Can we get you anything? We can stay as long as you want," Caitlyn said. Though she meant it, she immediately regretted her last statement. She didn't want Travis to think her life revolved around him.

Travis adjusted the blanket across his chest, and Caitlyn

noticed that his eyelids seemed heavy.

"We should go and let you rest." Caitlyn twisted her hair trying to ignore her disappointment.

Travis laid his head back and drifted off to sleep.

Caitlyn and Brittany left the room. In the hallway, they passed a young woman with long brown hair who gave them a polite smile.

"Do you know her?" Brittany said.

"I've seen her somewhere before, but I can't remember where," Caitlyn said.

They entered the elevator, and Brittany pushed every button. The doors closed.

"I can't take you anywhere," Caitlyn said.

"Maybe we'll meet some guy on one of the floors," Brittany said as she elbowed Caitlyn.

"Only you would think of scamming on a guy in the hospital."

"Isn't that what you're doing?" Brittany gave her a cheesy grin.

$$* \quad * \quad *$$

The spring day was a perfect mix of warm sunrays, soft floral scents, and cloudless skies. Caitlyn lay on her towel on one of the chaise lounges allowing the sunshine to dry her wet skin and listening to the music from one of her neighbor's apartment windows.

"Garrett is so hot in that swim suit. I could snuggle up to that body anytime. Whew." Brittany fanned herself.

"Here comes Darren," Caitlyn said.

Darren opened and then shut the gate. He made his way over to them. "Hi, Brittany."

"Hi, Darren. What's up?"

"Would you like to go out for dinner tonight?"

"Sure."

"I'll be over about 6:00 then."

Brittany smiled in her usual flirtatious way.

"See you later." Darren backed up a few steps, stumbled, and then turned around. He dropped his towel, peeled off his shirt, and dove into the water.

"Don't break his heart," Caitlyn said.

"Huh?"

"Do you even like him?"

"Sure." Brittany shrugged. "I like everyone."

Caitlyn rolled her eyes. "He was asking about you."

"When?"

"After we went to the movies. I saw him in the library."

"What happened?" Brittany scooted closer to Caitlyn.

"He asked if you'd go out with him again, and he had that I'm-totally-smitten-with-your-roommate look on his face."

"Hmm." Brittany raised her left eyebrow. "I've never thought too much of what the guys think or feel. I mean, I'm having fun and dating as many guys as I can."

"The salad bar thing." Caitlyn nodded.

"Exactly. Why settle for one when there are so many?" Brittany spread her hands out in front of her.

"You lecture me on being afraid to get involved with Travis, but I think you're just as afraid." Caitlyn pointed at Brittany.

"Of what?"

"Finding someone you really like. You go after so many guys because you're afraid of getting hurt." Caitlyn rolled over to her side and laid her head down. "I'm right and you know it."

* * *

Caitlyn sat in her apartment and absently surfed through channels. She wanted to visit Travis again but decided against it. She wasn't sure how she felt about him or how he felt about her. And she was still deathly afraid of risking her heart again. She wanted to be alone with her thoughts and try to make some sense of them.

The door opened slowly, and Hannah walked through. She gently closed the door behind her.

"Hannah?"

Hannah turned and Caitlyn could see her bloodshot eyes.

"What's wrong?"

Hannah took a few steps and fell onto the couch. She wiped at her eyes. "I've been thinking about what you said."

"Really?"

"I haven't stopped thinking about it since you mentioned it." She paused for a moment. "You're right. The temple is the only place to get married. I know that."

"Have you told Dave?"

"Not yet. I'm afraid he won't understand, and he'll break up with me. I love him."

Caitlyn reached over and hugged her roommate.

Hannah blew her nose. "I don't know what to do. Why did I fall in love with someone who couldn't take me to the temple?"

"He knows the Church is important to you, doesn't he?"

"I think so. I mean, I've never told him exactly how I feel because I didn't want to offend him."

"If you really love him, isn't it worth telling him how you feel? He might surprise you."

"I'm afraid."

"You can't be scared your whole life." Caitlyn blinked her eyes several times. Was she actually saying this? "Give Dave a chance, talk to him, and see what happens. But don't give in on your decision about the temple."

"What if he breaks up with me?"

"I guess, when we stop being afraid and take a chance, the risk is that we might get hurt." Caitlyn looked off into the darkness of the hallway.

Hannah squeezed Caitlyn tight. "Thank you. I'm so glad you're my roommate. You're great at giving advice."

"I am?"

Hannah gave Caitlyn another hug and then stood and walked toward her back bedroom.

Maybe Caitlyn should take some of her own advice. Travis hadn't ever given her any reason to think he'd hurt her, and it wasn't fair to compare him to Justin. Maybe it was time to stop being afraid and find out exactly what was going on with Travis and her.

sixteen

I thought it'd be nice to sign this card for Travis. He's having surgery on his leg tomorrow," Caitlyn said to the group gathered in her apartment. She spotted Chase and smiled, but hoped to avoid direct contact with him.

Caitlyn handed the card to Brittany who signed it and then passed it along.

"Since he won't be up to a visit tomorrow night, I think we should go by tonight and see him and that can be our FHE activity for the week," Caitlyn said.

"Sounds good to me," said Ethan who wore a blue BYU T-shirt.

"I'll even bake him some cookies," said Natasha.

"About 6:00, then? We can meet in the parking lot and carpool over there," Caitlyn said.

Most of the crowd headed out the door, but Chase stayed in the living room. Caitlyn mentally willed him to leave without saying anything.

Unfortunately, Chase didn't seem to pick up on her brain waves. He cleared his throat. "I can give you a ride over to the hospital."

"Thanks, but I'm planning to drive my roommates and the girls next door."

Chase half nodded.

94

"I'm sorry." Caitlyn shrugged.

They stood in awkward silence for a minute or so. Did she have to hit him over the head for him to get a clue? Chase finally said, "Would you like to go out on Friday? We could go miniature golfing."

"Miniature golfing?" Sounded too familiar.

"Yeah." Chase flipped his hair back.

Caitlyn furiously searched her mind for an acceptable excuse to avoid the date. "I'd really like to go, but I've got plans for Friday." Sounded lame, but it was the best she could do.

"Saturday?"

Was this guy dense or what? "Uh, why don't I get back to you later?" Caitlyn tried to smile sincerely.

"Okay." Chase gently kicked at the floor. He meandered over to the door and left the apartment. Caitlyn didn't want to be mean, but she didn't need any more complications.

✳   ✳   ✳

Caitlyn found a spot near her apartment complex under the shade of a large maple tree. She lay down on the cool grass and looked up through the thick leaves. Chase was a nice enough guy, but he didn't give her that pit of the stomach feeling simply by looking at her. He didn't take up residence in her mind and refuse to leave.

She rolled to her stomach and propped her head up on her hands. Travis made her forget who she was when he touched her hand. Somehow, he'd wrapped himself around her heart. She wanted to go see him and confess her feelings, but reality set in, and she decided to wait until the group went over at 6:00. She didn't want to seem overly anxious. After all, they'd only started dating less than a week ago, and there was no real commitment between them. Besides, she didn't want him to think she was interested, especially if he wasn't, unless he was, then she wanted him to think she was interested, if he'd like that.

Thinking of Travis made her mind turn into mush, so she

turned to her scriptures and decided to read. Today, even Isaiah would make more sense than her feelings.

* * *

The group piled out in the hospital parking lot. "I think this will cheer him up," Brittany said to Caitlyn as they galloped, arm in arm, across the parking lot.

"I'm sure he'll enjoy the cookies, too. I should've done that. If only I were a domestic goddess." Caitlyn hit herself on the side of the head.

Brittany stared at her.

"What?"

"You seem different tonight."

"What does that mean?"

"I don't know exactly. What did you do this afternoon?"

"Not much. Just read my scriptures. Isaiah writes so clearly, don't you think?"

"Huh?" Brittany shook her head.

"Never mind."

"I have a feeling you might want to stay a little later than the rest of us. True?"

"I don't know what gave you that idea."

"The way you're acting. You seem like you're in—"

Caitlyn reached over and planted her hand across Brittany's mouth. "I'll take my hand away if you promise not to say it."

Brittany nodded so Caitlyn took her hand away. "Love." Brittany shouted it and then ran toward the hospital doors.

* * *

Caitlyn poked her head into the room. "Travis?"

"Come in." He attempted to sit up a bit.

"Are you ready for some fun?" Caitlyn said.

"Absolutely."

The group filtered in.

Everyone took turns saying hello to Travis and asking how he was feeling. He kept nodding his head and smiling.

Natasha, the FHE sister with the cookies, handed him a plate. "We brought these for you. It's my mom's secret recipe." She smiled a little too big for Caitlyn's taste.

"Thank you. I think I'll like these a little better than the food here."

Caitlyn stepped forward. "We have a card for you, too." She handed him the envelope.

"Thanks."

"We wanted to come have FHE with you tonight since you'll be having surgery tomorrow," Caitlyn said.

"That'd be great." Travis ran his fingers through his hair and adjusted his hospital gown.

They sang an opening song, had a prayer, and then Jeffrey, one of the guys that lived in the apartment next to Travis, shared a few scriptures and a spiritual thought. They sang another song and then closed with a prayer.

"Thank you for coming. I appreciate it. These four walls seem to close in after a while," Travis said.

"Hope you feel better," Brittany said.

"Thanks, me too."

The group began filing out of the small room and into the hall.

"Does everyone have to leave?" Travis looked directly at Caitlyn.

Caitlyn glanced at Brittany, who said, "We can find a ride home. No problem." Brittany winked.

Caitlyn mouthed, "Thank you."

"Why don't you sit down for a minute?" Travis said.

Caitlyn sat in the padded chair next to his bed.

"I didn't think the entire FHE group would come by, but I'm glad they did. I feel better that we had family home evening."

Caitlyn smiled. "I like having FHE. We didn't do that in my family. My dad wasn't much for ever having church stuff at home."

"Because your mom is a member of the Church and your dad isn't."

"Wow. I'm impressed. You remembered about my family."

"I remember everything you've told me."

Caitlyn glanced down at the floor. She couldn't stop the smile that overpowered her face.

"Tell me more about your family."

"My mom went to church when she was younger, but then she met my dad and they got married."

"What church did he belong to?" Travis grabbed his hospital-issue cup and took a sip of water.

"He didn't really go to any church in particular. My mom decided she wanted me and my sister to have religion in our lives so one day she started taking us to the Mormon Church."

"How did your dad feel about that?" Travis's gaze intensified.

"He wasn't too happy about it, but he let us go. He never came with us, though. Mom would take us every week, but she never tried to get Dad to go or force him to let us do church things at home." Caitlyn crossed her legs.

"That must be hard."

"It is. Sometimes."

"It's good that you've kept going even though your dad doesn't support you." Travis took another sip of water.

"I had some good friends in my ward at home that encouraged me. They even got me to go to early morning Seminary."

"Friends are important."

"They are, but when it comes to a testimony, not even the best of friends can help you there. I had to work hard for my mine. But now it's my own, and no one else's."

Travis cocked his head and smiled. Caitlyn met his gaze and, in spite of her rapid heartbeat, gave him a confident smile.

They sat in silence for a few moments until Caitlyn said, "Has your family been here to see you?" She still wondered why Tanya had given her the North Pole treatment.

"Mom and Tanya were here earlier. They said my dad is on his way over. It'll be good to see him. He's awesome. We've spent a lot of time together tending the herd. I love working with my dad and the cows. Someday, I plan to run our family operation." His voice was soft.

"I guess that means you'll be a cowboy and have lots of little cowbabies?" Caitlyn emphasized the last word.

"Ah, you remember my comments about having a quiver full of kids?"

"Hard to forget. How many kids are in a quiver anyway?"

They both laughed.

Caitlyn glanced at her watch. "It's getting late. I better get back. I need my beauty sleep, you know." She fluffed her hair.

"I guess that's a matter of opinion," Travis said, and Caitlyn felt her chest constrict.

"You'll come by tomorrow?"

"Sure. After your surgery." Caitlyn stood.

Travis reached his hand out and took hold of Caitlyn's. "See you then." His touch made her muscles flinch.

The door opened, and Tanya walked in. She stared at Caitlyn and immediately moved her gaze down to their hands. "Am I interrupting something?" Her tone had an icy edge to it.

Caitlyn stepped away from Travis and said, "No. I was on my way out, anyway. Bye, Travis."

Caitlyn walked out into the hallway and waited for the elevator. What had she done to provoke Tanya?

She rode the elevator down to the lobby. As she was leaving, she noticed the same familiar girl with long brown hair that she'd seen the day before. An image of a group of people camping popped into her mind, but she couldn't make sense of it. Maybe this girl simply had one of those "familiar" faces.

*   *   *

Caitlyn threw open the front door to her apartment and spied Hannah and Brittany on the couch. "Hannah, we missed you at our FHE this evening."

"Sorry about that, but Dave and I had a talk this afternoon."

"How did it go?" Caitlyn asked.

"Not so well." Hannah wiped at her eyes. "I told him how I felt about the Church and that I wanted to get married in the temple."

"And?"

"He doesn't understand. He thinks we should get married now and worry about that later. He told me that if I loved him, I'd marry him without any conditions." Hannah looked at Caitlyn. "Maybe he's right."

"Hannah!"

"Calm down, Cait," Brittany said. "Maybe Hannah has a point."

"Are you serious?" Caitlyn shook her head hard and gave Brittany a wide-eyed look. She turned to Hannah and said, "You r need to think about this."

"I know, but I don't want to lose him."

"Didn't we talk about this?"

"Yes, but it was different when I talked to Dave. I love him, Caitlyn. I really do." She ran her fingers through her short blond hair

"I know and I understand how strong that feeling can be but think about the future. Do you want to get married out of the temple?"

Hannah buried her face in her hands and sobbed.

"Have you prayed about it?" Caitlyn said in a soft voice as she stroked Hannah's hair.

Hannah eked out, "No."

"If you pray about it, Heavenly Father will help you know what to do."

Hannah took a deep breath. She sat up straight and said, "You're right. I know you're right, but I'm not that strong."

"Yes, you are." Caitlyn gave Hannah a squeeze.

seventeen

Alison peeked under the tinfoil to make sure her specially prepared, oversized cinnamon roll was still in perfect condition. She flipped her long brown hair back behind her shoulders and opened the door to Travis's hospital room.

With her biggest smile, she said, "Hi, Trav. I brought you a surprise!" She unveiled the masterpiece. "One of my cinnamon rolls." She sashayed over to the bed and handed him the plate.

"Thanks, Alison. You certainly know my weakness," Travis said. He scooped some frosting on his finger and licked it clean. "You're an awesome cook."

"Thank you. The way to a man's heart is always through his stomach, right?" She caressed his arm and leaned in closer to him.

The door opened and Alison jumped back a bit. Tanya entered the room.

Tanya rushed to Alison and said, "Hey, best friend. Did you sneak something in to my poor little brother?" She gave Travis a pouty look. "Ooo. You make the best cinnamon rolls. Doesn't she, Travis?" Tanya looked at him and waited for a reply.

"Yeah, they're great." Travis tore a piece of the roll off and shoved it in his mouth. "This is delicious," he said with his mouth full.

"That's so attractive, Travis." Tanya took on a motherly tone. "Don't be rude in front of Alison."

"Sorry, Alison. Sometimes I forget you're not one of my sisters."

Sisters? What did he mean by that? Alison furrowed her brows. She certainly didn't want him to love her like a sister.

"You're like one of the family. And you spoil me like my mom," Travis said.

"Isn't that a good thing?" Tanya said as she stepped toward the bed.

"You bet." Travis ripped off another piece of the cinnamon roll.

"Hey, can you spare Alison for a moment? I want to get this recipe," Tanya said.

"No problem. I'll hang out right here," Travis said. He patted the bed with his hand.

Tanya grabbed Alison by the arm and pulled her into the hallway.

"What are you doing?" Alison said, not hiding her displeasure.

"Saving our plan."

"What are you talking about?" Alison jutted her chin out.

"Are you aware that another girl is coming to see Travis?" Tanya placed her hands on her hips.

Alison jerked her head back. "Seriously? I can't believe—"

"She's the FHE mom and Travis is the dad of their group at the apartments. I'm pretty sure she'd like to make it for real, too."

"What?" Alison said it louder than she intended.

"Her name is Caitlyn, and I saw her holding Travis's hand."

"Oh no, you didn't."

"Yeah, I did."

"Who does she think she is?" Alison paced the hallway fantasizing about slapping a girl she'd never met.

"Exactly."

Alison stood in front of Tanya. "What did he do?"

"Nothing. I'm sure he didn't know what to do. She's making moves on him while he's lying helpless in a hospital bed."

"What kind of a girl does that?" Alison heaved in a big breath and pushed it out. Her anger boiled.

"We need to remind him that he wants to marry you." Tanya pointed at Alison. "So what are we going to do about it?"

"I can't believe another girl is—"

Tanya interrupted and shook Alison a few times. "Listen to me, we need to concentrate on what to do. We have to put our plan into hyperspeed."

Alison waved her hand in the air. "I'm sure he doesn't like her. I mean, after all, we've been dating for years. It goes without saying we'll end up getting married. She's probably throwing herself at him, and he's trying to be polite about it."

"Even so, we can't let anyone, not even Travis, ruin our plan to be sisters, right?"

"You got that right. I plan to marry Travis, whether he likes it or not."

Tanya gave her a look.

"I mean, of course, he'll like it. It wouldn't make sense to get married if he didn't like it."

"We've planned this for too long to let some lame girl get in the way. What's the next step?"

Alison tapped her finger on her lips. She pointed her finger in the air. "I should be around a lot more often. I'll take time off work. And maybe if you keep talking about all of my good qualities, like my cooking, sewing, and all of my other domestic talents, he'll realize that I'm the one for him. It's only a matter of time before he realizes he wants to marry me."

"Now you're talking. I'll keep dropping hints about the two of you."

"I'll remind him of all the good times we've had. Which have been many, I might add." Alison closed her eyes and thought about her deep love for Travis. She'd loved him for so long, she couldn't remember not loving him. They were destined to be eternal companions with a brood of righteous children.

Tanya placed her arm around Alison and said, "Now, what about this Caitlyn girl?"

Alison raised her eyebrow. "Leave her to me."

"Sisters?" Tanya stuck her hand out.

"Sisters." Alison reciprocated the secret handshake they'd used since childhood. She felt sure that this girl offered no complications to her plan. She'd be Mrs. Alison Dixon in no time.

eighteen

Caitlyn tried to concentrate on her classes, but her thoughts kept wandering back to the hospital and Travis's surgery. How was he feeling? And, more important, how was he feeling about her?

Despite her best efforts, every time she saw Travis, her feelings for him grew stronger. Was it finally time to surrender and admit it might be love? No, it couldn't be. She'd only known him for a week and no one falls in love in a week. Right? Couldn't be love.

Someone coughed and Caitlyn glanced up. Her professor, with a disgruntled look on his face, held a paper out in front of her.

"Sorry." She cleared her throat.

"Seems your mind was elsewhere," he said in a nasal tone.

"I'm sorry."

"This is your most recent test. Please look it over."

She took the paper from his hand and said, "Thank you."

The score at the top of Thursday's test said it all. Travis was a distraction.

The class ended, and she gathered up her books and headed toward the Wilkinson Center to meet Brittany for lunch. As she crossed in front of the library she spotted Chase walking in her direction. She dodged inside the door and hurried to the east side to exit.

Just to be safe, she rushed from the library and entered the bookstore. She glanced over her shoulder to make sure Chase wasn't following her.

She made her way through the bookstore and was sidetracked by a display. Without warning, she ran right into someone, dropping her books with a loud thud. She leaned down to hurriedly collect her books without even glancing at who'd caused her embarrassing situation.

"Sorry about that," said a familiar voice. She shut her eyes while her body seized up in a paralytic stance. "Caitlyn? Is that you?" The muscles in her jaw involuntarily flexed.

She looked up. He still had his shiny blond hair and light blue eyes. He even had a tan. "Justin. What are you doing here? I thought you were still back home." She loaded her books in her arms and then convinced herself to stand and face him.

"My new father-in-law helped me decide to come up to school for summer term. Get this, he's even paying the bill for the whole thing. Pretty good, huh?" Justin gave a weak smile.

"I guess."

"I thought I'd look over the bookstore and get familiar with the campus. Kinda get settled."

Caitlyn nodded.

"I meant to call you. I feel bad about the way—"

"You ditched me at the temple?"

Justin kicked at the ground. He looked at Caitlyn and said, "I'm really sorry, Cait."

Caitlyn waved her hand in front of her. "Ancient history." Surprisingly, she meant it.

"I didn't mean for it to happen the way it did. I never wanted to hurt you. Really. I just didn't know how to tell you."

"I'm glad things have worked out for you." She studied him, waiting to feel sadness or anger or resentment or longing . . . or something but didn't.

"My wife, I still can't get used to that, will be here in a few minutes. You gotta meet her. She's the coolest."

"I'd love to stick around, but I'm late for a lunch date." So what if it was with Brittany; he didn't need to know that.

"Maybe we could get together."

She half nodded.

He bent down and picked up a book she'd missed. He handed it to her and his hand momentarily brushed hers. No rush of emotions. No electricity. No rapid heartbeat. She felt . . . liberated.

"Thanks. Good luck with everything." She smiled and triumphantly walked off.

She spotted Brittany at a table in the Cougareat and hurried over. She threw her books down and grabbed a chair. "You will never, ever guess who I just ran into, literally." She sat on the chair.

"Obviously someone you didn't expect."

"You got that right."

"Who?"

Caitlyn paused to build the suspense. "Justin."

Brittany's eyes almost popped out of their sockets. "Your ex? That Justin?"

"Yes, that Justin."

"What's he doing here?"

"He's going to school during summer term."

"Was his wife with him?"

"No, but get this, he wants to get together. And he apologized for how things ended."

"Really?"

"Amazing, huh?"

"Wow." Brittany shook her head. "That was completely random."

"This campus is huge and I have to be in the same place, at the same time, as Justin."

"How do you feel about seeing him?"

"Besides utter shock that I saw him, I don't feel anything."

"Serious?"

"Yeah, he handed me my book, and there was nothing, absolutely nothing, to his touch. I didn't feel a thing." She shrugged.

"Interesting."

"I used to feel all jittery when I was with him, but now, nothing."

"You must be over him."

"I think," Caitlyn held her hand up, "no, I know I am."

"And Travis?" Brittany said with a smirk.

"I haven't been able to concentrate on my classes at all today. I'm worried about his operation."

"Uh-huh."

"What?"

"You're over Justin because you're in love with Travis. I'm amazed it happened so fast, but your face says it all."

"You can't fall in love in a week. That's ridiculous."

"Keep telling yourself that." Brittany patted Caitlyn on the hand.

"I admit, I do have some feelings for him, but love? I don't know about that."

"I envy you."

"Why?"

"I wish I could feel that way and find someone to love."

Caitlyn reached across the table and laid her hand across Brittany's forehead. "Are you feeling okay?"

"Yes." Brittany removed Caitlyn's hand.

"Is this my salad bar roommate talking?"

Brittany played with her napkin. "I've been thinking about what you said the other day. You're right. I've never been with one guy long enough to let him hurt me. I go from one to the other so I don't have to worry about getting hurt."

"Go on," Caitlyn leaned in toward Brittany.

"Maybe it's time to get more serious."

"Wow." Caitlyn sat back against the chair. "Today is filled with surprises."

"What are your plans now? Going to see Travis?" Brittany asked.

"Maybe." Caitlyn checked her watch. "His surgery should be done by now, and he'll need to recover for a while."

"Maybe you can make friends with his sister." Brittany made a face.

"I don't get why she's been so rude to me."

"Probably feels protective. Once she gets to know you, she'll love you like I do."

*   *   *

Caitlyn stared at the red light, waiting for it to turn green. The song on the radio was the theme song of the movie she'd seen with Travis last week.

Now that she knew with a certainty she was over Justin, maybe it was time to move forward and take another chance. Travis wasn't Justin, and she didn't have any reason to believe he'd hurt her.

She couldn't deny the excitement she felt when she was with Travis. So what if it'd only been a week or so, her feelings were real, and it was time to stop hiding from them. Maybe she was falling in love.

She pulled into the parking lot and found a space. She gazed at herself in the rearview mirror and noticed the smile that broke at the edges of her mouth.

*   *   *

She gently opened the door to his hospital room and noticed a peaceful, sleeping Travis. She took a few steps inside and watched his rhythmic breathing. Even in his subconscious state, he made her heart do cartwheels. She wanted to rush over and spill out her feelings, but he needed his rest. Tomorrow would be soon enough.

nineteen

Caitlyn awoke to a pounding on the door. She wanted to sleep until it was time for class. She waited for one of her roommates to answer it, but whoever was on the other side continued to bang on the door. Obviously, she wasn't going to get any more sleep, so she rolled out of bed and dragged herself down the hall.

"Hold on a minute," she yelled.

She opened the door. A guy of average height and build with dark hair, hairy arms, and a five o'clock shadow stood there with a menacing look on his face. "Dave? What are you doing here so early? Where's Hannah?" Caitlyn stifled a yawn.

Dave brushed past her. "It's not early. And Hannah's at class." He planted himself firmly in the middle of the living room.

Caitlyn turned toward him. "Why are you here?"

"To see you." His voice was tight.

"Why?"

He narrowed his eyes and said in a low voice, "To tell you to mind your own business."

Caitlyn noticed his clenched fists and her heart rate doubled. "What are you talking about?"

"Hannah was set to marry me," he pointed his finger at Caitlyn, "until you had to butt in and confuse her. Now she says she won't marry me unless I take her to the temple. This wasn't an issue before you poisoned her mind." He glared at her. "I don't have to take her to some temple to prove that I love her."

Caitlyn blinked her eyes several times as she contemplated what to say to diffuse the situation.

"Marriage is marriage." He took a step toward her.

Caitlyn stood firm, refusing to allow Dave to intimidate her.

"You need to stay out of it." With his jaw set, he added, "I mean it. Leave Hannah alone and stop filling her head with all of your nonsense."

"It isn't nonsense."

Dave stepped closer to Caitlyn and shoved his finger in her face. "I say it is."

"If you really love her—"

"I do love her."

"Then listen to her. The temple is important—"

"Don't say another word. I've had enough of what you have to say."

"Ask her how she feels," Caitlyn said, hoping Dave would be reasonable.

Dave backed away from Caitlyn, his chest heaving. "Stay out of it." He spun on his heels and stomped out of the apartment, slamming the door behind him.

Caitlyn let out the breath she hadn't realized she was holding. She tried to control her shaking hands and the thudding in her chest. Dave was so angry, he seemed as if he wanted to hit her. How could Hannah want to marry someone with such a temper? She felt even more concerned than ever about her roommate.

*   *   *

Caitlyn attended her classes and then returned to her apartment for a long, hot shower. She picked through the pile of shirts on the bathroom counter and pulled one over her head. She heard the front door open.

"Anyone home?" came Brittany's voice.

"I'm in the bathroom," Caitlyn said.

"I thought you'd be at the hospital," Brittany said.

"I'm on my way. Do you want to come?"

The door opened again. Caitlyn heard Brittany say, "Hi, Hannah." Caitlyn swallowed hard. Had Dave talked to Hannah yet? Did he tell her about their confrontation?

Caitlyn adjusted her black and red striped shirt and stepped out into the hall. She took a deep breath and said, "Hey, Hannah."

"Where are you two going?" Hannah said.

"To the hospital to visit Travis," Brittany said.

"Travis?" Hannah said.

"He's our FHE dad, remember? He had the car wreck last week," Brittany said.

"I haven't actually met him."

"You should come with us. He's pretty cool, huh, Caitlyn?" Brittany elbowed her.

"Is something going on?" Hannah asked.

"No. Brit's being lame, that's all." Caitlyn gave Brittany a look. "You should come meet Travis."

They headed for Caitlyn's car and drove over to the hospital.

*　　*　　*

They arrived during dinnertime. Caitlyn spotted Travis's mom in the hallway. She approached his mom and said, "Hi. How is Travis doing?"

"Oh, hello, Caitlyn. He seems to be doing fine. The surgery went well yesterday."

"I stopped by last night, but he was asleep and I didn't want to disturb him." She felt a little sheepish admitting she'd come to see Travis. She didn't want his mom to think she was a stalker.

His mother said, "He's awake now." Caitlyn wasn't sure, but she thought she saw a glint of something in his mother's eyes.

Caitlyn, Hannah, and Brittany walked through the door into the hospital room. "Hey, Travis. Thought we'd drop by and see how you're doing," Brittany said. She sat on the chair next to the bed.

"I think I was, hmm, what did Grandma always say? 'Drug

through a knothole.' Yep, that seems to describe it."

"That good?" Caitlyn said.

Travis turned in Hannah's direction. "Hannah?"

Hannah nodded.

"Nice to meet you, daughter." Travis attempted a smile.

"Thanks."

"When will they spring you?" Brittany asked.

"Probably at the end of the week if everything looks good," Travis said.

"You'll be coming back to the apartments?" Hannah asked.

"Actually, my mom's decided I'm going back home. Something about recuperating." Travis pulled at his sheet.

Caitlyn's lungs grew heavy while the muscles in her stomach cramped. She cleared her throat. "You're leaving?"

Brittany cut in, "How can a father desert his children at a time like this?"

"A time like what?" Travis said.

"Um, I don't know, just a time like this." Brittany pleaded with her hands.

"You can try to convince my mom otherwise, but I think she's set on taking me back to Colorado."

A lump the size of a tennis ball formed in Caitlyn's throat while she struggled to control the tears propelling themselves to the surface.

"Can we smuggle anything in here? Food maybe?" Brittany asked.

"I'd love a chocolate shake," Travis said.

"Hannah and I will get you one. We'll be back." Brittany yanked Hannah out of the room.

"Can I interest you in a fine padded chair?" Travis looked over at the empty chair.

Caitlyn sat down. She couldn't find her voice to speak.

"Want to share my soup?" Travis offered a spoonful of murky white sludge.

Caitlyn shook her head. She gave a slight smile.

"I think they call it cream of something. I keep moving my

spoon around, but haven't come up with the something yet."

Caitlyn took a deep breath, regained her composure, and stood. "How about if I feed it to you?"

"I don't know if I can trust you. Are you a licensed soup-feeder?"

"Oh, come on, you're brave. Where's that daring, dive-from-the-bathroom-window-into-your-dorm-window side?" Caitlyn fed him a spoonful.

"Mmmm. Bland, tasteless, and otherwise unappetizing. Want some?" Travis smacked his lips together.

"Better not. I'm trying to cut down on my hospital food intake." She fed him another spoonful.

"Can we wait for the shake?"

"Your mom won't be too pleased if she finds out you're not eating your dinner." Her tone was more irritated than she wanted.

"It won't be forever, you know."

"What?"

"I'll be back up here in no time."

"I'm sure you will. Now, eat up." She shoved another spoonful into his mouth.

Caitlyn continued to feed him until Brittany and Hannah came through the door. Brittany pulled a shake from behind her back.

"I've heard you can do five years to life for bringing in contra-band to a hospital," Caitlyn said, working hard to hide her disap-pointment.

"I'll take my chances," Brittany said. She handed him the shake.

They all chatted for about half an hour until a middle-aged nurse with black curly hair came in. "You gals will need to leave. He needs his medication and the doctor will be by shortly."

"We'll see you later." Brittany and Hannah both waved and left the room.

Caitlyn's throat tightened as that same lump began growing again, threatening to choke her.

"See you tomorrow?"

"I think I have a test, and I'll need to do some heavy-duty

studying. Have a good night, though." She tried to say it as casually as possible.

She shuffled down the corridor. How could he leave when . . . what? What, exactly, was he leaving? She hated that his mother was probably right to take him home to recuperate.

In the parking lot, Brittany and Hannah stood by Caitlyn's car. "This isn't the end," Brittany said.

"He's going home. That's it," Caitlyn said with a shrug while her insides felt like they'd been puréed.

twenty

The next day, Caitlyn left campus and stared at the ground for most of the walk back to her apartment. It wasn't fair. She'd finally decided to open her heart again only to have it pulverized. The whole love thing was Hollywood hype and she didn't need it. She was foolish to have these feelings for Travis anyway. Who felt like this after only ten days? It was ridiculous.

She approached the common area of her apartment complex and heard a familiar voice call to her from the pool. "Hey, Cait, over here." Brittany waved her arms above her head.

Caitlyn shuffled over.

"Put your stuff away and come back out. It's a gorgeous day." Brittany leaned back against the chair with her face to the sky.

"I've got a project due tomorrow, and I need to work on it."

Brittany whipped her head up and gave Caitlyn a sad face. Caitlyn ignored her and continued toward the apartment. Brittany followed Caitlyn inside. "When are you going to see Travis?" Brittany asked.

"I'm not."

"You're giving up? Just like that?" Brittany stepped in front of Caitlyn.

Caitlyn pushed past Brittany and threw her books on the floor by the couch. She walked over to the cupboard and grabbed a cup.

She shut the cupboard door harder than she expected.

"There's nothing between us." Caitlyn filled her cup with water.

"If I can feel what's between you two, then I know you can. You're afraid to take a chance because there's a minor complication."

"He's going home to Colorado. That's more than a minor complication."

"Who's going to let a little distance get in the way?"

Caitlyn slurped the water in her cup.

"Let me guess. It's Justin again. He's made you afraid of every guy."

"He has not."

"Prove it."

Caitlyn glanced at the ceiling and then back down at Brittany. "Prove what?"

"Prove that Justin hasn't ruined your chance with Travis."

"Okay, I'll play along. How exactly would I prove that?"

"Go see him." Brittany pointed her finger at Caitlyn.

"But—"

"Get in your car and drive to the hospital." Brittany pulled Caitlyn from the sink area and shoved her toward the door.

"I don't want to do this."

"I wonder if you're more afraid that you'll get hurt again . . . or that you won't."

Caitlyn fluttered her eyelids. "Talking in riddles?"

"Nope. Simple truth. I think you're almost as afraid of it working out."

"Just because you're a psych major doesn't mean you know what you're talking about. Besides you should apply all of this to yourself."

"Go see him. Meet me at Burger Hut in an hour." Brittany opened the door, pushed Caitlyn outside, and shut the door behind her.

Caitlyn threw open the door and announced, "Justin has nothing to do with this." She shut the door.

* * *

Caitlyn's favorite song played on the radio, so she let the car idle in the hospital parking lot while she listened and stared out the windshield. She tapped her fingers on the dashboard and twirled her hair into a knot, something she'd done often since meeting Travis. She then had to spend a few minutes pulling out the tangle.

* * *

Caitlyn swallowed what felt like a jagged rock and took a deep breath. She poked her head into the doorway of the hospital room. "Hi, Travis."

"Caitlyn." The smile on his face broadened. "I'm glad you came by. Come in."

"How are you doing?" Caitlyn asked. She sat down in the chair and scooted it closer to the bed, immediately feeling the undeniable attraction.

"The doctor said I'm healing quickly. I'll be able to go home in a day or so." Travis's face showed his pleasure.

"That's good news." Caitlyn attempted to be cheerful.

Travis studied her for a few minutes. He asked, "Would you be interested in visiting Colorado this summer?"

The question caught her off-guard. "Excuse me?"

"Come see me."

Caitlyn sat back. This came out of nowhere. "I'm planning to go back home and work this summer." Though she wanted to shout her acceptance, she decided to keep her enthusiasm under control.

"You could stop by my house on your way home," Travis offered.

"I don't usually take the route to California by way of Colorado."

"You haven't heard?"

"What?"

"It's a new short cut."

"Oh, I see." Caitlyn nodded.

"Come on. It'd be fun. I'll let you shovel manure. And you can show me how you throw a hay bale. Only if you're up to it, of course."

"Sounds too good to pass up."

"You'll come?"

Caitlyn shrugged one shoulder. "I'll think about it."

"Hand me that paper and pen over there and I'll draw you a map."

As Caitlyn offered him the paper and pen, her hand brushed against his and the energy pricked her skin. She watched as he drew a map of his home and the surrounding fences and outbuildings. "This is the windmill north of the house. I used to climb it all the time. Has a great view of our whole place. You can see the mountains where we take the cattle to graze during the summer. I'll take you up there when you come." He winked.

"Heights and I aren't the best of friends. Besides you may not be climbing anything for a while." She pointed at his leg.

"Don't worry about that. You come and I'll show you a great time, I guarantee it." The magnetic gaze of his clear blue eyes locked with hers and a tingling sensation engulfed her. She didn't want the moment to end.

Without warning, the door opened and a girl with long brown hair wearing blue hospital scrubs sashayed into the room. She glided past Caitlyn and gave her an icy smile. Caitlyn recognized her as the same girl she'd seen a few times in the hospital. An image of camping popped into Caitlyn's mind. Suddenly, she remembered seeing the same girl in the photos at Travis's apartment when they met there for their first FHE meeting.

"How's my favorite patient?" the flat-faced girl said in a theatrical voice.

Travis cleared his throat. "Alison. I thought you were working."

"I am, but when I explained about your accident, my supervisor let me take some extra time for my break so I could check on you." She caressed Travis's arm and Caitlyn's stomach roiled.

"Alison, I want you to meet Caitlyn. She's the mother of our FHE group. I'm the dad." He pointed to himself with his thumb.

"How sweet." Alison pasted on a smile and said, "How nice of you to come by to visit." Her voice was like too much soda pop—sweet and sickening at the same time.

"Caitlyn, this is Alison," Travis said.

"Hi." A nauseating and all-too-familiar feeling overcame her. Déjà vu.

Alison gave a nod.

"We grew up in the same ward. She's working at the hospital in Orem," Travis said.

"Oh." Caitlyn forced a smile, wishing she could vanish. How did this happen again? How did she get sucked into caring about someone who had the same M.O. as Justin?

"I must tell you about Butch." Alison half-turned to Caitlyn and in a condescending tone said, "Butch is our bull. You know what a bull is, don't you?"

Caitlyn's face warmed. She eyed the window and contemplated jumping out of it. Was she the world's biggest idiot or what?

Alison turned back to Travis, "As I was saying, they aren't sure what to do with Butch. My mom says we should go ahead and butcher him and stick him in the deep freeze. I think she's tired of chasing him."

Caitlyn couldn't help but notice the spark in Travis's eyes when he said, "We had a bull like that once before. My dad was trying to get him in the barn one morning and he got halfway through the doorway and wouldn't budge. After two hours, my dad finally had enough and whacked him over the head with a two by four. Dropped that bull right where he stood."

Alison laughed. "Are you serious? Your dad did that?"

"He was spittin' mad when he had to go get the tractor and drag that bull out of the barn. We had our deep freeze full of that ornery bull for a long time."

Caitlyn shuddered at the thought of the poor, defenseless animal. She shuddered again at the thought of staying in the ever-shrinking hospital room.

Alison laughed and said, "I know exactly what you mean. You have to grow up on a ranch to understand this kind of stuff." She glanced in Caitlyn's direction.

Travis and Alison continued in their conversation and Caitlyn listened hoping to find an excuse to leave. She didn't have anything to add because, as Alison had indicated, she had absolutely zero knowledge of ranch life. The only obnoxious animals she'd dealt with were the cats that liked to crowd around her feet every time she ran the can opener. Besides, she wasn't sure she understood butchering animals, even if they were ornery.

Travis interrupted her thoughts, "Caitlyn, how was school today?"

"Fine. I—" she started.

Alison cut in, "Did you hear about Brother Simpson?"

Travis and Alison began another conversation. Alison hadn't missed a beat in trying to make Caitlyn feel like an intruder. Apparently, Caitlyn had garnered Alison's contempt.

After several minutes, Alison turned to Caitlyn. "So sorry. Trav and I forget when other people are around." She laughed, but it sounded more like a cackle.

Caitlyn couldn't stomach Alison's performance one more second. In a calm voice, she said, "I need to get back. My econ. book is calling my name." She stood.

"But—"

"Oh, Travis, let her go. She needs to study. Don't worry, Catherine, I'll keep Trav company."

Caitlyn gritted her teeth while she fantasized about wrapping Alison's stringy hair around her neck and choking the last breath out of her. And Travis? How dare he invite her to Colorado. Was she some kind of a fill-in for his girlfriend? She wasn't about to be Justin-ed again.

She exited the room but not before she caught Alison's glacial glare.

Caitlyn hurried down the hall to the elevator. She heaved in a breath while she waited. What a fool she'd been to think there was anything between her and Travis. Everything was crystal clear now.

*   *   *

Caitlyn's foot was heavy on the gas pedal as she navigated the back roads to the strip mall where Burger Hut was located. Her tires screeched when she stopped in the parking lot. She jumped out, slammed the door behind her, and ran to the entrance.

Caitlyn spied Brittany and rushed over to the table. She scooted across the booth.

"I already got your dinner." Brittany handed Caitlyn a bag. "How was the visit?"

Caitlyn unwrapped her burger but set it aside. Her churning stomach had destroyed her appetite.

"What happened?"

"He asked me to come visit him in Colorado."

"That's excellent." Brittany shoved a handful of fries into her mouth.

"Then his girlfriend walked in."

Brittany choked on her fries.

"I should have known. I should never have listened to you. I was right. They're all the same."

"Girlfriend?"

"She's from his home ward."

"Are you sure?"

"Absolutely. It was so obvious. I felt totally lame sitting there."

"I don't get it. You said he invited you to Colorado to visit him."

"He did."

"You must be wrong about this girl."

"Alison. That's her name. Doesn't it sound like fingernails on a chalkboard?" She gagged.

"You're in love with Travis." She pointed at Caitlyn.

"I am not." Caitlyn sat back.

"You wouldn't be flipping out about this Alison if you weren't. You have to do something."

Caitlyn shook her head. "Nope. I'm really done now."

"You can't give up."

"This conversation is over. I need to study." She stood. "I'll see you back at the apartment." Caitlyn grabbed her uneaten hamburger and the bag and tossed them into the trash can on her way out.

Caitlyn started her car. She blared the radio and rolled down the window. The spring air blasted her face as she drove back to her apartment. Brittany didn't know what she was talking about. It was bad enough he was going home, but another girl? Not again, her heart couldn't take it.

Maybe, for a millisecond, Travis had wrapped himself around her heart, but she was an experienced unwrapper.

twenty-one

Caitlyn sat on her bed. She hadn't seen or talked to Travis since her discovery that she wasn't the only one competing for his attention. All day long she had tried, unsuccessfully, to unwrap him from her heart. Maybe she wasn't as experienced at unwrapping as she thought.

She doodled Travis's name on one of her notebooks. She crossed it out. She wrote it again and then scratched it out. One more time, she drew the letters to his name and then promptly scribbled out each one. She argued internally about going to visit him, but decided she couldn't deal with the Justin thing all over again.

She cracked open her economics textbook, but every other word seemed to spell Travis. She laid her head on the thick book. Suddenly, she lifted her head to view her clock radio. It was after 6:30 p.m. and visiting hours would be over by 8:00fShe desperately wanted to see Travis. Tomorrow he'd leave the hospital, and her life, forever.

She glanced over at the mirror hanging on the wall. "What should I do?" she said. She gazed at the mirror waiting for an answer until the door swung open.

"Admiring yourself again?" Brittany asked.

"I thought maybe I'd give myself some answers."

"Here's an answer for you. If you don't go see Travis, you'll regret it." She wagged her finger at Caitlyn.

Brittany flung herself on the bed. "Don't let this Alison girl get in your way and don't let him go home without saying good-bye."

"I don't—"

"This situation is completely different from what happened before."

Caitlyn leaned back. "Let's recap. I think I have a relationship with Justin, in fact we're engaged. Until what? Oh, yeah, I find out there's another girl and not only does he dump me the day of our wedding, he marries her instead. She becomes me and has my wedding. Sounds eerily familiar, don't you think?"

"I thought you were over Justin."

"I am, but I'm not over how much he hurt me, and I'm certainly not in the mood to repeat it. Once was more than enough."

"So you're going to make a decision about Travis based on Justin?"

Caitlyn said nothing.

"And in your warped mind that makes sense, right?"

"It does to me. Who needs a guy anyway? I can be completely happy on my own." Caitlyn crossed her arms in front of her chest.

"Who says Travis will hurt you?"

"It's bound to happen. If Alison has her way, they'll be married within a month. She's probably already picked out her wedding dress and silverware."

"And if she doesn't have her way?"

"You don't understand." Caitlyn emphasized her statement with her hands.

"Why? Because I've never dated anyone more than a couple of times and you think I've never been hurt by a guy?"

"Well . . ."

Brittany drew in a deep breath. She sat up straight and said. "When I was a senior in high school, I met Landon shortly after he got home from his mission. I was so in love with him. We dated for a few months and the way he talked, I thought we were going to get married. I had my wedding all planned out in my mind. I couldn't imagine being with anyone but Landon."

Caitlyn jerked her head back. "I had no idea. What happened?"

"He took off for school and never called me again. I was destroyed when I realized he'd left me. I still don't know what happened, but I vowed, like you, to never get seriously involved again."

"You never told me."

Brittany brushed the air with her hand. "Old news. But, watching you has made me realize how lame we both are."

"You might be lame, but I'm not."

"We're both letting past relationships rule us. We're each reacting a different way. You told me the other day that I was afraid. You're right. I am."

Caitlyn nodded.

"I'm so scared of being dismissed again, that I haven't let myself get very involved with anyone. That's why I go from guy to guy, I guess. But, we're both going to end up miserable if we aren't willing to take a chance."

Caitlyn moved in closer to Brittany. "You really think so?"

"Yeah, I do. Travis has feelings for you. It's so obvious I'm sure Alison can tell, too. Maybe she's obsessed with him; you know a fatal attraction thing."

Caitlyn gave Brittany a look. "What do you think I should do?"

"Go see him. He's a great guy and he's beautiful." Brittany squeezed Caitlyn's arm. "You'll never find love if you're afraid. Don't think about it, just go."

*   *   *

Caitlyn stood in the hospital corridor a few feet from Travis's room. Maybe Alison was his past. After all, he'd asked Caitlyn to come see him in the hospital and now he'd invited her to come see him in Colorado. She took a few steps toward the doorway. Maybe she'd been too hasty in her judgment of his relationship with Alison. She took another step and peeked in.

"Come in," Travis said as he motioned with his hand.

"I wanted to say good-bye. I hope your trip home goes well and your leg heals quickly." Caitlyn wiped her moist hands on her jean shorts.

"Come sit down."

She moved the chair close to his bed and sat.

"You're going to come visit me in Colorado, right?"

Caitlyn shifted her weight in the chair.

"If you're really nice, I'll even teach you how to milk a cow." Travis winked.

"You mean squeeze those things on the cow and make milk come out?"

"They're called teats, and they're attached to the udder. And, yes, that's what I'll teach you." Travis laughed.

"Sounds kind of disgusting to me."

"Nothing's better than fresh, warm milk right from the—"

"Okay, stop right there." Caitlyn held her hand up. She was beginning to feel that her fears were unjustified.

Travis laughed. "City girls."

Caitlyn attempted to slug him on the arm, but he grabbed her hand. His touch sent involuntary ripples through her body.

"You'll enjoy Colorado. A walk along the river right before sunset is so relaxing." He caressed her fingers.

"Sounds nice."

Travis stroked the back of her hand, and she felt a connection she'd never felt before. It was as if they were all alone, suspended in time . . . until the door opened and Alison appeared. Immediately, Travis dropped Caitlyn's hand. He cleared his throat and said, "Alison, what's up?"

"I wanted to see you. What time are you leaving in the morning?"

"As soon as the doctor releases me, I reckon." Travis rubbed his fingers together.

Caitlyn's stomach flip-flopped, and her cheeks burned. She wasn't sure if she should be angry at Alison for interrupting or at Travis for throwing her hand down. Confusion and anger welled up inside. Perhaps her hasty judgment was right after all.

Alison sauntered over to the bed, ignoring Caitlyn. "How are you feeling?" She placed her hand on his, the same hand that, seconds before, had been holding Caitlyn's.

"Pretty good for having a broken leg, crushed ankle, and imbedded glass in my arm and forehead. Other than that I'm perfect."

"Hmph," Caitlyn said under her breath.

"You're always so funny." Alison touched him on the arm.

She turned to Caitlyn, finally acknowledging her presence, and said, "How nice of you to visit again. You seem to be here all the time. You're really magnifying your calling, aren't you?"

"Uh . . ." It was all Caitlyn could mutter before Alison turned back to Travis.

"Now, I told my mom to be sure and bring you some of her apple pie that you always gobble up when you're over at my house."

Travis adjusted the blanket and shifted his weight in the bed.

"I'll be home soon and then I'll give you all the TLC you need. I've decided to spend the summer at home." She didn't look at Caitlyn, but Caitlyn could still feel the arctic attitude.

"I'm sure your family will enjoy that," Travis said. He sat up a bit.

Alison glanced at her watch. "I snuck out on my break to see you. I couldn't go to bed tonight without making sure you're doing okay. I'll be back in the morning. See you then." She squeezed his shoulder.

"Uh, thanks for coming by." Travis adjusted his covers again.

Alison walked to the door. She turned around and over-smiled at Travis. For a moment, Caitlyn fantasized about running across the room and knocking all those teeth out of Alison's mouth. She chuckled to herself.

After Alison left, an awkward silence filled the room. It hung over Travis and Caitlyn like a thick, early morning fog. Neither of them said a word for several minutes.

Finally, Caitlyn broke the silence. "Uncomfortable?"

"A little." Travis blew out a breath.

Caitlyn held up her bare wrist. "Hmm. Will you look at the time? I better get going."

"Will I see you before I leave tomorrow?"

"I have classes in the morning." Her voice was void of all emotion.

"I'll call you when I get home."

Caitlyn gave a nod and left the room.

*   *   *

Caitlyn was in self-preservation mode while she trudged through the parking lot. She yanked her car door open and flopped herself inside. She sat in her car staring at the dimly lit entrance to the hospital. Why had she listened to Brittany? Obviously, there was something between Travis and Alison or he wouldn't have thrown her hand to the ground. And Alison had made it more than clear that she wanted Travis. So where did that leave Caitlyn?

*   *   *

She parked her car and then walked into her apartment. Brittany was lying on the couch, snoring. She didn't want to wake her because then she'd have to strangle her.

After her prayer, she climbed into bed. She lay on one side and then rolled to the other. She turned again onto her back. She pulled the covers up to her chin and then kicked them off. She sat up.

Thoughts swirled in her mind. Travis seemed to be interested. The connection she felt was undeniable. So why did he react like that when Alison entered the room? Could she trust Travis or was he Justin in disguise? Too many questions bombarded her mind and confusion settled heavily in her stomach.

She studied the pattern of moonlight as it sifted through the mini-blinds on her window. It was quiet in her apartment, but she could hear muffled voices outside near the pool area. She leaned back and stared at the ceiling.

The clock counted minutes that felt like hours. Should she visit him in the morning? Could she not visit him and live with that? What if Alison was there? Far too many complications.

She made her decision.

twenty-two

Caitlyn's eyelids fluttered open and she struggled to focus her gaze. The clock read 8:37 a.m. Only twenty minutes until her first class. She burst out of bed, snatched a pair of jeans from the heap of clothes on the floor, and poured herself in. She yanked a purple shirt out of the half-opened top drawer and flung it over her head.

"A little late this morning?" Brittany sang out as Caitlyn rushed into the bathroom area.

"I don't know how I overslept. I must've turned off my alarm. This is not a good day to be late."

"Tell me what happened last night."

Caitlyn shot her a look. She squeezed toothpaste onto her toothbrush and stuck it in her mouth.

"He called me," Brittany said.

"Huh?" Toothpaste foam oozed out of the corners of her lips.

"He wants you to come see him before he leaves and asked me to convince you."

"I can't." Caitlyn wiped at her mouth with the back of her hand.

"Or won't? What happened last night?"

"I don't want to get into it right now." Caitlyn replaced the toothbrush and started brushing again. She scooped some water from the faucet and rinsed out her mouth. She smiled at herself in the mirror.

"If you don't go see him, you'll regret it." Brittany pointed at her.

"I don't think so. You said the same thing last night, and you were completely wrong."

"How so?"

"I guess he neglected to mention how he was holding my hand—"

Brittany interrupted, "Cool."

Caitlyn continued, "Until Alison came in the room and he threw my hand to the ground." Caitlyn reenacted the event.

"Ouch." Brittany held her hands up.

Caitlyn grimaced.

"I'm sure there's a good explanation."

"Yeah, he and Alison are still together. I finally decide to open myself up and, wham, I get knocked flat." Caitlyn swiped her arm across the space in front of her.

"Even if they are still going out, which I doubt, you can deal with a little competition."

"I don't want to." Caitlyn tugged at her hair.

"Maybe he's worth it."

"Maybe he's not." Caitlyn said it with as much conviction as she could.

"You'll never know unless you try."

"I'm not up to this. I can't do the other girl thing again. I learned my lesson from Justin."

"Cait," Brittany pleaded.

"I thought about it over and over again last night, and I decided it was better to put him out of my mind."

"But—"

"I need to concentrate on school anyway, and you're making me late." Caitlyn started down the hall. Over her shoulder she added, "Besides, I'll be going home for the summer in a few weeks and none of this will even matter."

*   *   *

Caitlyn slid into her seat only seconds before class began. She listened as best she could and took a few notes, but her mind kept slipping back to the hospital. If she went to see him again it would only lead to heartache and she didn't need that. So what if she'd momentarily let herself feel a strong something for Travis? It was a mistake she planned to rectify. Anyway, he'd be happy with Alison and all their little cowbabies. She'd be happy with . . . well, she'd be happy graduating from college and going on with her safe, painless life. Or something like that.

Even if there was still a tiny part of her that cared about Travis, and even if it seemed like he cared for her, it was better to get out while she still could. She wanted to forget about the whole thing.

She strolled across campus and gazed up at Mt. Timpanogos. The tallest peaks still wore snow and were a stark contrast against the blue sky. She let out a long sigh. If only she'd never accepted her calling to serve as the FHE mom, then she wouldn't feel this way. It was the bishop's fault. No, it was Alison's fault. If she'd only minded her own business and stayed away, then things would be different.

In reality, though, she had to shoulder all of the blame because it was her own fault. She knew better than to get involved with another guy. If she'd learned anything at all from Justin, it was that relationships equaled a broken heart.

Caitlyn hung her head down and studied the cement walkway as she made her way toward the Wilkinson Center. She heard a familiar high-pitched voice call out her name. She lifted her head and saw Brittany standing in front of her car waving wildly.

"What are you doing?" Caitlyn shouted.

"Coming to get you. Jump in and I'll explain." Brittany ran over, grabbed Caitlyn's arm, and pulled her toward the Wilkinson Center parking lot.

"What's wrong?" Caitlyn picked up her speed.

They reached the car. Brittany opened the door and shoved Caitlyn inside. Brittany raced around to the other side of the car, opened the door, and jumped in. She slammed the door. They both buckled their seat belts and Brittany whizzed onto the street.

"What's going on?" Caitlyn said.

"You'll see."

When Caitlyn recognized the route, she let out an exasperated breath. "Why are we going to the hospital?"

"I'm not going to let you mope around the rest of the term because you were too stubborn to go see Travis. He called again, and I told him you were coming by."

"You did what?" Caitlyn faced her roommate.

"Don't make me a liar."

"I don't need to."

"Come on, Cait. Don't be lame."

"I can't believe you're kidnapping me and making me do this." Caitlyn folded her arms and let out a grunt.

"You'll thank me someday."

They pulled up to the curb. Brittany undid her seat belt, threw open her door, ran around to Caitlyn's side, and flung the door open. She reached in, undid Caitlyn's seat belt, and yanked Caitlyn out of the car. "This is for your own good. Travis wants to see you. Don't you get it?"

"But—"

"Who cares if he went out with Alison or a hundred other girls? He wants to see you. Now, go up there and see him." Brittany gave Caitlyn a shove and then got in the car.

Caitlyn stared at the hospital while Brittany drove away. Her heart beat feverishly. She placed one foot in front of the other and forced herself to walk into the lobby.

Caitlyn stared at the open elevator.

"Are you going up, miss?" an elderly man asked from behind her.

"Oh, uh, no. Go ahead." She stepped out of his way.

The older man shuffled into the open elevator. She watched the doors close. Her heart seemed to slip down into her stomach, and she wanted to make a dash through the front doorway. The elevator doors opened again and she stepped inside.

The ride up was faster than she'd hoped, and when the doors opened, she saw Travis's mother and Tanya at the nurse's desk. She inhaled deeply, exhaled through her mouth, and crossed her fingers. She hoped Alison wouldn't be in the room when she walked in.

She closed her eyes for a moment and then took the first step into his room "Hey, Travis." Her voice was light.

"Caitlyn, I'm glad you came by. I'm about to check out." He was sitting in a wheelchair with his right leg propped up.

"I'm sure you'll be glad to get out of this place." She nodded.

"You're telling me." He grinned and goose bumps erupted on her arms.

"We all, the FHE group and me, hope you feel better." She cleared her throat.

He took her by the hands and pulled her close to him. He gazed up into her eyes and said, "I'm glad you came by. I wanted to talk about what happened last night."

"Last night?"

"When Alison came in and I—"

"Couldn't drop my hand fast enough?" Caitlyn gave him a quick smile.

"It's not what you think. I want you to come see me this summer. I'll call you when I get home. I—"

"Excuse me," said a nurse. Travis turned his head and Caitlyn slid her hand out of his. The nurse continued, "I'll need you to fill out this paperwork. The doctor is down the hall speaking with your mother. He'll be in to see you momentarily." She handed Travis a clipboard.

Caitlyn stepped back and out of the door. "Good-bye, Travis," she whispered, feeling like she'd left a crucial body organ in his room.

She boarded the elevator and Tanya slipped in beside her. "It was nice of you to come see Travis," Tanya said. "I told Alison how you've taken your calling so seriously and visited Travis a lot. She appreciates it because she hasn't been able to see him as much as she wanted with her work schedule."

Caitlyn didn't say anything.

"You don't need to worry, though. I'm sure Travis will be up and around in no time, especially after Alison gets home and takes care of him."

Caitlyn nodded and wondered why the elevator ride was taking longer than her entire drive back to California.

"I've always known they'd end up together," Tanya said with a small laugh.

Finally, the elevator stopped and the doors opened. Caitlyn turned to Tanya, "It was nice to meet you." Caitlyn gave her a smile and walked out through the lobby. Apparently, Tanya wasn't aware that Travis had invited her to come visit, or was she? Caitlyn couldn't quite figure out Tanya.

In the parking lot she spotted Alison. Suddenly, her face felt warm, her jaw tightened, and her stomach throbbed.

With a smile like a used car salesman, Alison said, "Oh, Catherine. How nice of you to come see Travis."

"It's Caitlyn."

"Oh, so sorry. Have you seen Trav?" Alison tousled her long, stringy hair.

"I did. He's ready to go home." Caitlyn kept her voice even.

"Only a few weeks and I'll be able to give him everything he needs. He'll be recuperating all summer. His mom told me that I'm the only one she'll allow in the house because he needs his rest. You understand, don't you?"

"Oh, I understand."

"It was nice meeting you, Cath, I mean, Caitlyn. I'm sure Trav appreciates all of your hard work. You take care of yourself." Alison gave her a curt smile and sashayed into the lobby.

Caitlyn stomped out to the parking lot and spied Brittany's car. She quickened her pace until she reached it. She opened the front door, slid across the seat, and stared out ahead of her.

"So?" Brittany said.

"I'd like to kill her.

"Her?"

"I saw Alison, and she's asking for it. I'd like to pull every hair out of her head. Who does she think she is? I should—"

Brittany interrupted, "I thought you didn't care—"

"Don't talk. Drive." Caitlyn narrowed her eyes, but she could still feel Brittany's gaze. "What are you smiling about?"

"You're infected with the Travis virus."

"Do you sit around and think up stupid stuff like that?"

"Nope, it just comes to me." Brittany waved her hand in the air.

Caitlyn rolled down the window.

"What happens now?" Brittany asked.

"I have no idea."

twenty-three

Caitlyn tallied the hours since Travis's departure. By her calculation, he should've arrived home already and should be calling soon. He'd said he'd call when he got home, right? Though she had plenty of homework to keep her busy, she knew she wouldn't be able to concentrate. She wanted to chill on the couch, eat popcorn for dinner, and stare at the TV while she waited for his call.

She heard a loud knock. Her roommates were scarce so she walked to the front door and opened it.

"Hey, Caitlyn."

"Uh, Chase." Caitlyn coughed a couple of times. He sauntered into the apartment and stood next to the dining room table.

He combed his fingers through his blond hair. "How about a movie tonight?"

"It's Friday."

Chase nodded. "You're worth a Friday ticket."

"Actually, I'm really tired and I have a bunch of homework this weekend. Finals aren't too far away." Caitlyn forced a smile.

"Is that a no?"

"Well . . ."

Chase stepped toward the living room. "We can watch TV instead." He walked over to the couch and sat on it. "Sit down." Chase patted the cushion next to him.

Caitlyn's feet were glued to the floor. She silently argued with herself for a few moments because she didn't need any more complications.

Chase patted the couch again.

Caitlyn took a few steps and sat toward the other end of the couch. She glanced over at him while he watched the television. He wasn't bad looking, and he was polite, both good qualities. He dressed well and didn't have bad breath. His hair was nice. He seemed to be interested in her, but all she could think about was Travis.

She heard the voices of her roommates a split second before they burst through the door.

Brittany stopped in her tracks. "Chase? How's it going?"

"Do you guys want to watch *The Fugitive* with us?" Caitlyn said.

"Harrison Ford is still hot for an old guy, but I need to—" Brittany started to say.

Caitlyn jumped up and grabbed Brittany. "Here's a seat on the couch for you. And, Hannah, sit down. I'll get the popcorn."

Brittany and Hannah exchanged looks.

Chase didn't notice much of what was going on. He seemed entranced with the movie.

Caitlyn brought over the popcorn and handed the bowl to Hannah. "Oh, you know what, I've got this big test on Monday and I need to study. It was good seeing you, Chase." She gave a short wave as she walked backward down the hallway. She ignored the looks from her roommates.

He grabbed a handful of popcorn and said, "I guess I'll see you later then."

She felt guilty dumping Chase on Brittany and Hannah, but she didn't want to spend another minute in that suffocating room. She couldn't deal with the idea of Chase wanting to date her or the pounding silence of her cell phone.

A half an hour later, her door flew open. "Thanks for making us babysit Chase," Brittany said. Hannah was right behind her.

"I have to study for a test. Sorry."

"Getting a lot of studying done?" Brittany asked.

"Actually, no. I can't seem to focus."

Brittany sat on the bed. "Has Travis called yet?"

"No. And thank you for bringing that up." Caitlyn shut her book.

"Maybe they didn't drive straight home," Hannah said. She sat on the edge of the desk.

"Or maybe he didn't feel up to it. I'm sure he'll call tomorrow," Brittany said.

A loud knock at the front door interrupted their conversation. "I'll get it," said Brittany. She jumped up and ran out of the room.

Caitlyn could hear Brittany say, "Wait a minute and I'll get her."

For a moment, Caitlyn held her breath, but she reminded herself it couldn't be Travis. She hoped it wasn't Chase again.

Brittany peeked her head into Caitlyn's room. "Hannah, it's Dave."

"What does he want?" Hannah's face took on a white hue.

"To talk to you," Brittany said.

"I haven't talked to him since I told him I only wanted to get married in the temple."

"Don't give in," Caitlyn said.

"We'll be right here if you need us," Brittany said.

Hannah stood, paused for a second, and walked out of the room. Caitlyn could hear Hannah and Dave begin a conversation. She shut the door.

"Why did you do that?" Brittany said.

"It's rude to eavesdrop." Caitlyn sat on her bed.

"But she might need our help." Brittany lay on the floor.

"Hannah has to make this decision on her own. I hope she makes the right one."

"It's amazing that you feel so strongly about temple marriage considering—"

"I got dumped the day of mine?" Caitlyn said.

"No. Because your dad isn't even a member of the Church."

"He's a good man, just blind when it comes to the Church."

She stopped for a moment. "I decided a long time ago, after one of my Young Women leaders said we should write out our goals, that I wanted a different kind of marriage than my parents have. I want to be sealed in the temple." She glanced in the direction of the living room and asked, "What do you think they're talking about?"

"We could open the door and listen." Brittany's eyes grew large.

"Brit!"

They heard the door shut.

"Hannah?" They both said as they rushed out of the bedroom.

"What did he want?" Brittany said.

"He wants to work things out. He doesn't want to give up on us," Hannah said.

"And?" Caitlyn said.

"I used all of my strength and told him that unless he wanted to investigate the Church, we didn't have anything to work out."

"You did?" Brittany said.

Hannah turned to Caitlyn, "What you said about your dad . . . I knew I had to take a stand because I do want a temple marriage."

"How did he react?" Caitlyn said remembering her own experience with Dave.

"He was angry," Hannah said. "But after he calmed down, he said this wasn't about the Church, that it was about us being together and getting married. He doesn't understand." Hannah wiped at her eyes.

"How did you leave things?" Brittany said.

"I told him I wasn't going to change my mind. He tried to hug me, but I wouldn't let him because I was afraid I'd cave in. He was pretty mad when he left."

"Wow," Brittany said. "You're strong."

"Caitlyn helped me." She smiled at Caitlyn. Her voice quivered as she said, "It really hurts, but I know it's the right thing to do."

"How about ice cream?" Brittany said.

Hannah brushed the tears from her cheeks.

"Let's hop in my car and we'll go get a half-gallon and sit around with spoons until it's gone or we're puking our guts out. Kind of a celebration slash depression party," Brittany said while she looked over at Caitlyn.

twenty-four

Caitlyn awoke and attempted to clear her mind. She finally realized that it was Saturday morning.

She meandered into the kitchen for a late breakfast of a few crackers, lumpy yogurt, and stale bread. Time to get a few groceries. She checked her phone. If only it'd ring. She squinted her eyes and focused all of her energy on it. Ring, will you? Please? Just a little, tiny ring? She shook her head and said to herself, "This is driving me insane."

She headed for the shower. A trip to the library would help her catch up on some assignments and take her mind off the thundering silence of her cell phone.

After a long afternoon of accomplishing nothing, she walked into the apartment, pulled her phone out of her pocket, and threw it on the floor. "You stupid phone, why don't you ring?"

Brittany emerged from the hall.

"I didn't know you were home," Caitlyn said.

"I'm guessing Travis hasn't called."

"Nope."

"Don't freak out. He'll call."

"He better." Caitlyn picked up her phone and stomped off to her room.

*　　*　　*

The lessons in Relief Society and Sunday school were well-prepared but didn't engage Caitlyn's mind. She was elsewhere. In Colorado, to be exact.

He said he'd call. It had been almost two days and nothing. Why hadn't he called?

One of the girls from the apartment downstairs played the prelude music for sacrament meeting.

"Is anyone sitting here?" Chase asked, pointing to the chair next to Caitlyn.

Caitlyn looked behind, in front of, and under the chair. "Doesn't look like it."

He laughed. "You're funny." He edged by her and sat down.

Caitlyn didn't say anything. Chase leaned over and whispered, "You gave a good talk a few weeks ago."

"Thanks. Has it only been a few weeks? Feels more like a few months."

"I was thinking, maybe—"

"Oh, there's Brit." Caitlyn waved her roommate over.

"Hey, guys, what's up?" Brittany sat down.

"Nothing," Caitlyn said.

Chase cleared his throat.

Caitlyn turned back to Chase and said, "Oh, sorry, were you saying something?"

"I was . . . well . . . no."

Caitlyn let out a breath of relief and looked over at Brittany who was smiling.

Darren sat in the seat next to Brittany, and Caitlyn noticed a different look in her flirty roommate's eyes.

The meeting began. Caitlyn tried to focus on the talks, but her mind wasn't cooperating. Maybe Travis didn't make it home. Of course he did. Maybe he'd been sleeping a lot. For two days? No, it was something else. Maybe he got home, decided he didn't want anything to do with her, called Alison, and they ran off and got married. No, there wasn't enough time for that. Was there?

Caitlyn rested her head on her hand as sacrament meeting seemed to drone on.

"Are you okay?" Chase asked. He placed his hand on her shoulder.

"Small headache, that's all." She sat back against the chair. Chase lifted his hand.

After sacrament meeting, Caitlyn couldn't leave fast enough. She wanted to hurry back to the apartment just in case her phone was ringing. She hitched a ride with one of the girls who lived in the apartment next door to hers.

Inside her apartment, she rushed to her phone to check for a voice mail or text message from Travis. Nothing. She slammed the phone shut and made her way to her bedroom to sleep off the rest of the day.

twenty-five

$\mathcal{M}$onday morning. It was, by far, the worst day of the whole week and meant she had a boatload of assignments and tests ahead of her. Since she hadn't heard a word from Travis, this Monday morning would definitely rank up there as one of the five worst of her life. She made her way to the bathroom and examined herself in the mirror.

She heard her cell phone ring. She froze in place while her nerves sizzled. *Could it be?* It rang again. She convinced herself to move and raced into her bedroom. She didn't even check the caller ID before she flipped the phone open.

"Hello," she said in a rough, early-morning voice.

"Caitlyn?"

A tingling sensation started in her stomach and traveled up her spine to the top of her scalp. "Travis?"

"Sorry to call so early."

"No problem, I've been up forever. Remember, I'm up with the rooster? Oh, no, that's you." She combed her fingers through her tangled hair and gave a nervous laugh.

"Do you have a minute?"

"Sure." She concentrated her efforts on maintaining a calm voice.

"I wanted to call and see how you were doing."

"Doing great, thanks." She twirled her hair so tightly around her finger, it jerked her head from the phone.

"The ride back was a rough one, that's why I didn't call until now. I had to go see the doctor on Saturday."

"Is everything okay?"

"Yeah, but I have to take it easy for a while. I want you to come visit, but it'd probably be better to wait a bit."

Caitlyn swallowed her disappointment. "Okay."

"I'll call you when I'm feeling better and we can make a plan."

"I hope you feel better."

"I'll see you soon." She could almost see his gorgeous face and mesmerizing blue eyes.

"Bye." She clutched the phone to her chest and took several breaths. Maybe he did care about her.

"Who was that?" Brittany said as she walked into the bedroom in her fluorescent green pajamas.

Caitlyn closed the phone. Though she tried to stop herself, a smile broke out across her face.

"Serious?" Brittany let out a scream. "I told you he'd call."

"Maybe you were right and maybe . . ." Caitlyn grabbed Brittany; they embraced, and jumped up and down together.

twenty-six

Caitlyn finished packing her car. Her finals hadn't been as hard as she'd feared, though it'd be a miracle if she passed her economics class. The last few weeks had been intense trying to study and finish projects and papers.

As she walked back to her apartment for a few last things, her thoughts centered on Travis. She had hoped to visit him before returning home for the summer. Unfortunately, he hadn't called for more than three weeks so she assumed he wasn't feeling up to a visit.

"Looks like that's it," Brittany said, looking around Caitlyn's room.

"I guess I'll be on my way then. You'll keep the apartment in good shape until I get back?"

"Of course. I wish I could go home, but since my parents are traveling all summer it makes more sense for me to stay and work."

"Be back before you know it."

"I'll miss you," Hannah said.

A knock sounded at the door. Hannah stepped over to open it. Caitlyn noticed a funny look on Hannah's face. Hannah opened the door wider, and Chase walked in.

"Hi, Caitlyn," Chase said.

Brittany and Hannah headed toward the hallway. Caitlyn gave them a pleading look, but they left the room.

"Are you going somewhere?" Chase said.

"I'm on my way home for the summer."

"I've been trying to get a hold of you." He flipped his hair back.

"I'm sorry. I've been so busy with school and packing to go home. Did you need something?" She tried to sound sincere.

"No, I guess not. Are you coming back in the fall?"

"That's my plan."

"Maybe I'll see you when you come back." Chase smiled. "I'll be in the same apartment."

Caitlyn nodded.

Chase left and Caitlyn shut the door. Chase didn't make her skin feel like it was on fire or make her heart beat so fast she thought it might explode. He didn't occupy the corners of her mind or cause her to twist her hair into knots. Most of all, he wasn't Travis.

Hannah and Brittany emerged from the back bedroom.

"What're you going to do?" Brittany said.

"I'm sure he'll forget all about me over the summer."

"Besides, Travis is the man," Brittany said. She did a dance around Caitlyn.

Caitlyn gave her a look. She glanced at the clock and said, "I better get on the road. It's a long drive, and my mom is way stressed about me driving by myself." Caitlyn opened the front door and walked out.

Brittany and Hannah followed her out to the parking lot where they exchanged hugs.

"See you in a couple of months," Caitlyn said.

"You better call when you go see Travis. And don't leave out any of the juicy stuff, either." Brittany said, rubbing her hands together.

Caitlyn gave a half-smile and opened her car door. She got in, put on her seat belt, and started up the engine. She watched Brittany and Hannah disappear in her rearview mirror.

twenty-seven

The drive was long, lonely, and filled with desolate scenery mile after mile after mile. The desert didn't hold much attraction. Caitlyn pictured the beach in her mind. With each mile, she became more anxious to swim in the ocean and walk along the shore, squishing the cool sand between her toes. She could almost smell the moist sea air.

She was excited to see Lindsay and her parents. She was a bit apprehensive about her dad because she knew he'd try to talk her out of going back to BYU for another year since his plans didn't coincide with hers. Caitlyn wanted to graduate from BYU and, if she ever did get married, marry someone in the temple. Her dad's plan included her graduation from the local university and marriage to someone that'd provide a decent living and be good to her, but not necessarily LDS. In fact, he'd told her more than once that he'd be deeply hurt if she excluded him from the wedding ceremony, a weight she'd carried even before the defunct engagement to Justin.

She gazed toward the changing hues of the horizon as day turned to dusk. What was Travis doing? Was he thinking about her?

She pumped up the volume on the radio and sang to the songs to keep herself awake through the lonesome night. Finally, after more than twelve hours, she drove down the familiar street she'd lived on since she was a small girl.

She turned off the engine and exited the car. She stretched her arms and legs and massaged the kink in her neck. Before she reached the door, it opened and Lindsay greeted her.

"Cait!" Lindsay flung herself at her older sister.

"Hey, Linds." They hugged each other.

Lindsay stepped back. "Glad you got here. Mom's been worried you might get hijacked by terrorists or take the wrong turn and end up in Mexico or something."

Caitlyn's mom, dressed in jeans and a dark blue shirt, walked up behind Lindsay. "How about a hug?" She and Caitlyn embraced. Her mother said, "I'm so relieved you're home. Driving by yourself isn't safe, you know."

"I know, Mom," Caitlyn said.

"You've done something to your hair," her mother said as she examined Brittany's handiwork.

"My roommate talked me into it. The streaks are pretty light, I know."

"It reminds me of when you were younger, after a summer at the beach. I like it."

"You've changed your hair, too. I like it short." Caitlyn touched her mom's soft hair.

"Do you like the color, though?" Her mom scrunched up her hair.

"Yeah. Now we're both a little blonder."

Her mom gently tugged Caitlyn toward the family room. "Come sit down. I'll make you something to eat."

Caitlyn sat on the leather couch and Lindsay plopped down next to her. "Whatever happened to that Travis guy? Is his leg better?" Lindsay scooted closer to Caitlyn.

"He's in Colorado, recuperating."

"Are you a couple?" Lindsay flipped her long, wavy brown hair behind her shoulders and flashed a big grin.

Caitlyn cleared her throat. "I wouldn't say that, exactly."

"Why not?"

"I haven't heard from him in a few weeks." Caitlyn made a pouty face.

"So where do you stand?"

"He invited me to come see him in Colorado."

"Cool."

"He said he'd call when he was feeling better. Hopefully, it'll be soon. You know how I hate waiting."

"I hope it won't be too soon, though, so we can hang out."

"I'm planning some serious beach time, believe me," Caitlyn said.

"By the way, Mr. Jackson called a few days ago to make sure you're planning to start work on Monday," Lindsay said.

Caitlyn laid her head back against the couch. "Real life ruins fantasy beach life once again." She sighed.

"I'm glad you're home, Cait."

"Me, too. How come you're up so early on a Saturday morning?"

"We have a temple trip. We're meeting at the church in a little while. I could skip it if you want." She braided her hair in a side braid.

Caitlyn held her hands up. "No way. I loved doing baptisms for the dead."

"Dad isn't too thrilled about it."

"Is he ever?"

Lindsay shook her head. "I'll be home about 4:00 or so. Of course, with L.A. traffic it could be later."

"Have fun."

Lindsay gave Caitlyn another hug and trotted down the hall.

Caitlyn's nose recognized the fragrant bacon scent. It'd been too many boxes of cold cereal since her last visit home at Christmas. She jumped up, walked into the kitchen, and sat at the light oak table.

"You look good," her mom said while she scrambled some eggs in the frying pan.

"This smells delicious," Caitlyn said. "Where's Dad?"

"He had an early morning meeting with one of his big new clients."

"Oh."

"This particular client has been somewhat demanding lately. He was audited and is having your dad go through all of his files, paper by paper." Her mom reached into the cabinet and pulled out a small glass. She placed it in front of Caitlyn.

"It's good some people enjoy accounting. Not me. Way too boring. When will Dad be home?"

"He said he'd wrap it up as soon as possible so he could get home and see you," her mother answered. She handed Caitlyn a plate filled with eggs, bacon, and toast.

Caitlyn inhaled deeply. "Sure is good to be home."

After Caitlyn offered the blessing, her mom asked, "How did you do on your finals?"

"Fine, I guess. Things took an unexpected turn."

"Travis? Is that his name?"

"Yeah."

"He's the one that was the dad of your FHE group, right?"

"Yep." Caitlyn took a sip of juice, and it dribbled down her chin.

Her mother handed her a napkin. "You said he was obnoxious."

"He was, at first. But, when I got to know him, he was pretty amazing."

"He had the car accident?"

"Uh-huh."

"You like him that much?" Her mother leaned against the counter.

"I do. I think he might even be . . . the one." Caitlyn used her fork to move the eggs around on her plate. "I know I planned to marry Justin and I was devastated when he left me, but now I'm glad he did because I wouldn't have met Travis."

"I see," said her mom.

Caitlyn munched on a piece of bacon. "He wants me to come to Colorado."

"Colorado? That's so far away. I don't think you should drive—"

"It's all happened so fast. One minute he's totally on my nerves, and the next . . . Do you really think it could be love? Can you fall in love this fast?" Caitlyn grinned as she thought about Travis.

"Well—"

She looked at her mom and her smile faded. "You think I'm on the rebound."

"I didn't say that."

"Then what?"

"You were involved with Justin for so long—"

"And this has happened so fast, you think it can't be love?"

Her mother raised her eyebrows.

All of a sudden, Caitlyn's doubts about Travis crashed down on her. "Maybe you're right."

* * *

Caitlyn dragged herself up the stairs and down the hall to her soft yellow bedroom. The room was still decorated with her tennis posters, photos from high school, and memorabilia. She plopped down on the bed and flung herself back. She stared at the ceiling and wondered if she was being ridiculous. Would Travis call?

All the familiar sights and smells filled her room. She could hear the garbage truck making its stops through the neighborhood while the moist sea air slipped gently through her open window. Without warning, though, her eyelids slammed shut.

* * *

"Knock, knock. Time for dinner," her mother said.

Caitlyn sat up and shook her head. Her mother stood in the doorway. Caitlyn focused on her and said, "Dinner? How long have I been asleep?"

"About nine hours."

"Really?"

"I wanted you to get some rest. I figured you were exhausted after finals and the long drive home."

"I didn't mean to sleep this long." She shook her head again.

"What are we having for dinner?"

"Tamales."

"Mmm, my favorite," Caitlyn said.

"I know." Her mom winked.

*   *   *

Caitlyn sat on the couch. She heard the garage door opener and jumped to her feet, eager to see her dad. She hoped they'd have a nice dinner together and not discuss anything controversial.

The door opened, and her dad stepped inside. He removed his sunglasses and set his leather briefcase next to the door. "Caitie!"

"Hi, Daddy."

He pulled her close into a bear hug. After a few moments he said, "Let me take a look at my college girl."

Caitlyn smiled.

"I see you have a new hair style."

"A little different color in places. Looks like you might have a little streaking going on yourself."

"Makes me look distinguished, right?" They embraced again.

Arm in arm they walked over to the dining room table.

"You two sit down. Lindsay called and Sister Bailey is bringing her home in a few minutes," her mother said.

"Glad you're home, Caitie. Any problems?" her dad asked.

"Nope."

"I told your mom you'd be fine, but you know how she prefers to worry," he said with a teasing smile.

"I heard that," her mom said from the kitchen.

He ran his fingers through his thick, curly hair. "How did you do on your finals?"

"Okay. I think."

They both sat at the table. Her father said, "You're a good student. Have you thought about my suggestion?"

Caitlyn rolled her eyes. So much for staying away from a controversial subject.

"Well?"

"Dad, I love BYU. I don't want to attend another school."

"You'd be closer to home."

"I know, but—"

"I have a young man I'd like you to meet."

"Dad—"

"He's the son of my new client. He recently graduated with honors from UCLA and is planning to attend law school."

"I'm not—"

"I'd like to invite him for dinner some night soon. Give him a chance. You'll like him."

Caitlyn breathed in deeply. Her father meant well, he always meant well, but he didn't, or wouldn't, understand her goal to marry in the temple. "Is he a member of the Church?"

Her dad nodded. "I think he goes to church."

Caitlyn raised one eyebrow. "The LDS Church?"

"Now that I'm not sure about. We didn't get into religion. But his father thought it'd be a good idea for you to meet his son."

Caitlyn's mom entered the dining room. "Robert, will you give the girl a break?" Her mom rested her hand on Caitlyn's shoulder.

"She needs to get out and meet some young men. After all, that Justin is married now."

"Dad, I have met someone."

"Oh? Who?" He poured some lemonade into his glass.

"His name is Travis Dixon, and he's from Colorado. Didn't Mom tell you?"

"Not that I recall. What else do you know about him?"

Caitlyn grinned and said, "He's amazing. He wants to take over his family's ranch."

"What?" The tone in her father's voice communicated his disdain.

"His family raises cows."

"Now, don't be silly, Caitlyn, you wouldn't be happy with a hick from Colorado."

"He isn't a hick. And he's LDS."

"You know," he took in a breath, "I've gotten used to you going to church, but it seems a bit discriminatory to limit yourself to members of the Mormon Church. There are plenty of decent, prospective young men out there who aren't Mormon."

"I really don't want to get into this again for the millionth time. Can we just eat dinner?"

Lindsay opened the front door. She stepped halfway in, waved her hand, and said, "Thanks," over her shoulder. She walked into the house and closed the door. She looked in the direction of the dining room table. "Who died?"

"No one. Dad and I were talking, that's all," Caitlyn said.

"What's for dinner?" Lindsay said.

"Are you going to change out of your dress?" Caitlyn asked.

"I wasn't planning—"

"I'll help you." Caitlyn popped up.

"What're you doing?" Lindsay said, almost tripping as Caitlyn pushed her up the stairs.

Caitlyn whispered, "Dad was bugging me about Travis."

"Did he call or something?"

They reached Lindsay's room and Caitlyn sat on the bed. "No. Dad was asking about him."

"Dad was pretty mad when you were engaged to Justin and he couldn't go to the ceremony. He complained about it all the time. He's still talking about how the Church is prejudiced against fathers who don't go to church."

"I know. He doesn't get it. If he'd give the Church a chance, maybe he'd feel different."

Lindsay patted Caitlyn on the shoulder. "I'll let you pave the way for me so when it's my turn he'll already be used to the idea."

"Thanks. Of course, I may end up never getting married." Caitlyn rubbed her face.

"Why do you say that?"

"I don't know. I guess I'm overly anxious for Travis to call so I can go see him."

twenty-eight

"How was your first day at Kids Kamp, honey?"

Caitlyn reached over and grabbed a few slices of cucumber out of the large bowl.

Her mother slapped at her hand. "Stop picking at the salad."

Caitlyn sat on the barstool. "The kids were a little hyper, but the beach was great. I think I got sunburned, though." She hurried and grabbed a chunk of avocado from the salad while her mom rummaged through the refrigerator.

"You had a phone call today," her mom said as she returned to the salad with a bell pepper in her hand.

"I did?" Caitlyn gave a loud sigh and said, "Finally. Weird that he called here instead of my cell. I wonder how he got this number." While her heart pumped quickly, those same, familiar feelings rushed over her body and held it hostage as she thought about seeing Travis again.

"It was a young man."

"Travis." A smile erupted across her mouth.

Her mother didn't reply.

"Mom?"

Her mom shook her head. "It wasn't Travis."

"Serious?" Disappointment smacked her in the face.

"It was Eric Anders."

"Who?"

"I think he's the son of your dad's new client."

"Oh." She inhaled deeply and then let her breath out slowly. "What's wrong?"

Caitlyn covered her face for a second. She removed her hands and said, "I don't understand why Travis hasn't called. He said he would. I really want to go see him. I don't get it."

"Maybe—"

"And I'm so not interested in meeting this Eric guy." Caitlyn snatched a piece of lettuce from the salad. "Why does it have to be such a big pain in the—"

"Caitlyn!"

"I'm going to my room."

*   *   *

The next several days passed even slower than finals week while Caitlyn waited for Travis to call. She walked into the family room after an extra long day of chasing kids at work.

Her dad was seated in his brown leather recliner. He looked up from behind the newspaper and said, "Eric has called here several times, but you haven't returned any of his phone calls. He says you're not answering your cell phone."

"I've been busy with work." Caitlyn sat cross-legged on the love seat across from her dad.

"I think you're avoiding him, and I don't understand why." Her dad placed the paper on the floor.

Caitlyn rolled her eyes. "Do we have to talk about this?"

"My client is wondering why his son isn't good enough for my daughter."

"It isn't that, Dad. I'm waiting for Travis to call."

"Travis?"

Caitlyn nodded.

"You mean, the kid from Colorado?"

"Yeah." Caitlyn twisted her hair.

"Don't you think if he were interested he'd have called by now?" her father said.

Her dad said out loud what she'd been thinking for the past two weeks.

"Eric wants to take you out. You should give him a chance."

"Dad, I don't want to." Caitlyn emphasized each word.

"Is this about Eric not being Mormon?"

Caitlyn didn't say anything.

"You were engaged to Justin, a Mormon missionary. He left you the day of the wedding. Now, this Travis, another Mormon boy, has left you, too. Maybe it's time to look elsewhere."

Caitlyn shook her head as she pursed her lips to keep them from quivering.

"Isn't it true?" Her dad peered at her.

Caitlyn covered her eyes with her left hand. Anger and sadness churned inside her. Her father was right.

"Why are you waiting for someone who isn't going to call when there's a nice young man with a future ahead of him that wants to take you on a date?"

Caitlyn clenched her teeth, trying to compose herself. She removed her hand from her eyes. "You don't understand, Dad."

"Why are you wasting your time waiting for someone who isn't interested?"

"Thanks." Caitlyn stood.

"Caitlyn, wait. I'm not trying to upset you." He reached his hand out for her.

"Could've fooled me." She wiped a tear from her cheek.

"I'm trying to make you see that you need to move on."

Caitlyn couldn't deny her father spoke the truth, but it cut her so deeply she could no longer listen to him. She left the room.

She lay on her bed and hugged a small throw pillow. Time to face the truth. Travis wasn't going to call. Whatever they had, if anything, was over. He'd made that painfully obvious by his lack of contact. She'd been waiting for a call that wasn't coming.

The door to her bedroom opened slightly. "Caitlyn?" her dad said.

"Yes?"

"I didn't mean to hurt you. I'm sorry."

"It's okay, Dad."

He sat on the edge of her bed. "I want you to be happy, that's all."

"I know. You just don't understand."

"Try me."

"Are you going to actually listen to me?" She turned to her dad.

He nodded and said, "Yes, I'll listen to what you have to say."

"I don't know how to make it any clearer, but I'd rather be alone all of my life than marry outside the temple."

He cocked his head to the right. "You don't mean that."

"Yeah, Dad, I do."

"But, why? Why would you give up marrying someone simply because it isn't in one of your temples?"

"Because I want to be married for this life and the next."

"I know the Mormons teach that kind of thing, but that doesn't make it true." He pointed at her.

She gently placed her hand across her chest. "I know it's true, in here, and I know I won't be happy any other way."

"How can you be so sure?"

"I've prayed about it. Just like I've prayed about Joseph Smith and the Book of Mormon."

Her dad shifted his weight on the bed. "We've had this discussion before and—"

"You've taught me to have my own mind. I haven't been brainwashed or forced to believe any of this. I've prayed about it and made my own decision. I know for myself it's true."

"I admit the Mormon Church has some good qualities, but so do other churches. To make the claim that it's the only true church is a little arrogant, in my opinion. And for you to sacrifice so much for it is foolishness."

Caitlyn's face was hot and her pulse raced. It was the same discussion she always had with her dad and with the same outcome. He refused to open his heart and listen to the truth.

"Besides, as I told you before, I don't think much of a church that prohibits fathers from attending their daughters' weddings."

"You can go to the temple. All you have to do is join the Church."

He gave her a look that tore into her heart. "I think you need to accept reality, in more ways than one."

Caitlyn's lips trembled.

"This Travis boy isn't going to call, and you need to get on with your life. Forget about him."

The lump in her throat threatened to cut off her air supply, and her heart felt like mincemeat. Was it because her father was right about Travis or because, once again, he'd made it clear he wasn't at all interested in the Church?

twenty-nine

The waves gently lapped against the shore while the seagulls dove down periodically to gather morsels left on the sand. The sun was beginning its descent below the horizon. A few wispy pink-colored clouds spread thinly across the sky. The cool water washed between Caitlyn's toes and left pockets in the sand.

The beach always offered solace for Caitlyn. In a few days, she'd be leaving to return to BYU, against her father's wishes, again. At least he'd relented about her dating his client's son, and she'd avoided any dates with him.

She hadn't heard a word from Travis all summer. Even after she'd summoned up her courage and sent him a get-well card, there'd been no response. No matter how she turned it over in her mind, she couldn't make sense of it. She'd felt such a strong connection with Travis, and it seemed as if he'd felt it, too. He'd wanted to see her in the hospital, and he'd invited her to come visit. It all pointed to them getting together. But now, more than two months later, all she had were aching memories.

She wandered along the beach at the edge of the water. Maybe she'd been wrong about Travis. He must not be the one. For all she knew, he was already married to Alison. She clenched her fists. That name still felt like the wet sand that caught in her bathing suit and irritated her skin until it was raw. She picked up a piece of driftwood and flung it out toward the waves. Alison's image cankered her mind. She let out a long, mournful sigh.

thirty

"ow do I look?" Alison spun around for her roommate, Jessica.

"Beautiful. But I thought you were only going to the mall."

"We are. Travis should be here any minute." Alison adjusted her pale blue shirt and straightened her flowing print skirt.

"It was nice of him to help you move back up here, crutches and all." Jessica munched on an apple.

"That's the kind of guy he is." Alison hugged herself.

"What happened while you were home?"

"I worked at the hospital in town but went over to his house almost every night. For the first few weeks, he was pretty out of it. He even had to go back to the hospital a couple of times because he had an infection. We went out several times after he was feeling better."

"Are you engaged?"

"Not officially. I think he's waiting to be totally recuperated before he asks me." Alison fluffed her hair. "While we're at the mall, I'm going to gently guide him into a jewelry store."

"Sounds like you've got it all planned out."

Alison grinned. "You have no idea."

*　　*　　*

"I'm not sure the mall is such a great idea with these crutches, Alison."

"Oh, come on, it'll be fun."

Travis smiled. "Mall and fun don't really belong in the same sentence do they? Shopping gives me a headache."

"Men." Alison raised her hands up in the air.

Travis maneuvered his way through the mall.

"Let's look in there." Alison pointed to Zale's Jewelry store.

"Why?"

"For fun, of course."

"Why don't I sit on this bench, and you can go look."

Alison sighed. "I'll be back in a minute."

She walked over to one of the counters and gazed at the shimmering rings. She was intoxicated by the glittering diamonds.

"May I help you?" a man in a grey suit and glasses asked.

"Can I try on that ring?" She pointed to a large solitaire pear-shaped diamond with smaller diamonds surrounding it.

The salesman handed her the ring and she slipped it on her finger. She stretched her hand out in front of her and admired the ring. Pulses of happiness surged through her.

"Do you like it?"

"I love it. It's perfect. My fiancé is sitting on the bench out there. I'm going to bring him back in and show him this ring. It's definitely the one I want."

Alison returned the ring and turned around. Travis was standing and talking to a guy and a girl. Alison hurried to the group.

"Hello," Alison said, interrupting their conversation.

"Alison. Do you remember my roommate, Darren?" Travis said.

"Of course. We met a few times. How nice to see you again." Alison smiled sweetly.

"This is Brittany. She was Caitlyn's roommate," Travis said.

"Caitlyn?" The name chewed on the edges of her nerves. She didn't want to let on that she remembered exactly who Caitlyn was. She shook her head. "I don't recall anyone by that name."

"She was the mother of our FHE group. You met her in the hospital," Travis said.

The memory of Caitlyn trying to steal Travis assaulted her mind. Of all the people at the mall, why did they have to see friends of the one girl who had tried so desperately to ruin Alison's plans? She shrugged. In her most innocent voice she said, "Sorry, don't remember. Now, Travis we don't want to be late for our dinner reservations, do we?"

She wrapped her arm around Travis. "So nice to see you again, Darren. And nice to meet you, Brittany." She gave a short wave.

As they walked down the mall, Alison determined to erase any memory of Caitlyn from Travis's mind. No one would thwart her plans, especially not some empty-headed city girl who had no idea how to make someone like Travis happy.

thirty-one

The drive back to Provo hadn't changed much. It was still long and boring. The radio and a few of Caitlyn's favorite CDs kept her company through the night.

She pulled into the parking lot of her apartment building about mid-morning. It was good to be back, and she was excited to see Brittany and find out what had happened with Hannah over the summer.

"Hey, Cait," Brittany shouted across the parking lot as Caitlyn opened her door. She didn't bother to shut the door as she ran to meet Brittany. They hugged each other.

"How was your summer here? I mean, after all the phone calls and texts you sent I have a pretty good idea." Caitlyn gave her roommate a sarcastic look.

"About that, I meant to call you, but I've been a little busy."

"With what?"

"Remember Darren?" Brittany's smile swallowed her face.

"Vaguely."

"We've been dating all summer, and I think he might be proposing this weekend." Brittany clapped her hands.

Caitlyn's mouth fell open. "You're getting engaged?"

"Kinda."

Caitlyn slugged Brittany in the arm. "Are you serious? I can't believe you didn't tell me. You're almost engaged, and I'm the last to know."

"I should've called or texted you about it. I didn't expect it at all. It just kind of—"

Caitlyn grinned. "I'm happy for you."

"Really?"

Caitlyn nodded.

"I guess that blind date way back during spring term was a pretty good one," Brittany said.

Caitlyn shook her head. "Darren must be pretty amazing to make you want to settle down. What a miracle."

"What are you talking about? I've always been a one man woman."

"Yeah, right." Caitlyn coughed several times.

They walked toward their apartment each holding a box. Brittany said, "How was your summer?"

"The beach was great, and my job was fun. Lindsay and I got to hang out."

"Anything else? Like trips to Colorado?"

"Hmm, let me see. Nope, don't remember any."

"Didn't Travis call?"

They dumped the boxes in Caitlyn's bedroom.

"Travis? The name is somewhat familiar, but, no, don't recall contact with anyone named Travis. Sounds like the name of a big loser anyway. Ancient history."

"Are you sure?"

"Completely. In fact, he's such ancient history they've already written about him in the history books." Caitlyn let out a laugh. "I'm hilarious." Caitlyn opened the box with her bedding and threw it on her bed. "Why?"

"Oh, I don't know."

Caitlyn studied Brittany. "Why do you have such a weird look on your face?"

"I do?" Brittany scrunched up her face.

"What are you hiding?"

"I don't know what you're talking about." Brittany pulled a pillowcase from the box.

"Brit?"

"Okay, okay. I sort of saw him at the mall."

Caitlyn took a deep breath in an attempt to calm the loud pounding in her ears. "You saw Travis?"

"Yeah. I was with Darren, and we ran into him at the mall. He was still on crutches."

"Did he say anything?"

"He was about to say something but—"

"What?"

"Someone interrupted us."

"Who?" She clenched her teeth in anticipation of Brittany's answer.

"Remember, I'm only the messenger."

"Okay. Out with it."

"It was that one girl."

"Alison?" Caitlyn said it through her teeth.

"Yeah, that was her name. He introduced us."

"Is that so?"

"Now, Cait."

"I knew it. They're probably married. She had it all figured out. That's why she was so rude to me at the hospital. I never had a chance. I'd like to . . ."

"Wait a minute. They aren't married. I know that."

"But they're together."

"Kind of looked that way. When he explained who I was, she put her arm around him. I don't think—"

"Please, I've heard enough. He can marry Alison and have lots of cowbabies and drink milk straight from the cow and do that farmer thing for the rest of his life. I don't care at all. Not one tiny bit. I'm over him."

"That's obvious," Brittany said. She rolled her eyes.

"Really. I don't care, and I don't want to talk about it anymore."

"But, Cait." Brittany tried to protest.

"You know, I've got to unpack these two boxes and my car before I go get the rest of my stuff from storage. Thanks for your help." She pushed Brittany out of her bedroom, shut the door, and threw herself on the bed.

How could he? He promised to call and never did. She waited all summer to hear from him and all the while he was with Alison. What a loser. The more she thought about it the more she wanted to rip something, or someone, apart. She thrust the door open and stomped into the kitchen.

"I thought you didn't care." Brittany flipped a cracker in her mouth.

"I don't."

"Call him."

Caitlyn spun around to face Brittany. "What?"

"Give him a call. Maybe things aren't what they seem."

"Call *him*?" Caitlyn pointed to herself. "Me, call him? That's as likely as snowboarding at the beach."

"Maybe you'd feel better."

"I'll tell you what'd make me feel better. Calling him and telling him what a jerk he is." Caitlyn placed her hands on her hips. "Making me wait all summer for his phone call."

"Do it. You've got his number, don't you?"

Caitlyn reached into her purse and pulled out her wallet. She took out the carefully folded piece of paper that Travis had used to write his address and draw the map to his house. She unfolded it and stared at the phone number.

"He said he wouldn't be here until winter semester. He must still be living at home."

Caitlyn fingered the paper.

"Travis made sure to tell us that he'd helped Alison move back here. Honestly, I think she was trying to make me think there was more going on. I'm not sure they're really together."

"Doesn't matter. He left me hanging all summer. You convinced me to stop being afraid and to believe in him. All that got me was a long summer of nothing."

"I don't care what you say. I still think there's a chance."

Brittany sat on the counter.

"Why would you think that?"

"The way he looked at me."

"What?"

"It was almost like he wanted to ask about you, but Alison walked up before he could say anything."

Caitlyn pointed at Brittany. "He had all summer to call me and say something."

"You should call him. Seriously."

Caitlyn chewed on the inside of her bottom lip while she contemplated the idea of calling him.

Brittany ripped the paper out of Caitlyn's hand.

"Brit, wait."

"For what?"

Brittany flipped open her phone and began dialing the phone. "Hi, is this Travis? . . . It's Brittany, Caitlyn's roommate . . . Fine, thanks. Can you hang on a minute?" She handed the phone to Caitlyn.

Caitlyn refused to take it. She held her hands up and said, "I don't want to talk to him."

"Tell him what you think."

"I can't do that."

"Yes, you can." Brittany shoved the phone in Caitlyn's face.

"Fine. You win." Caitlyn took the phone. "Hello?"

"Caitlyn?"

His voice made her throat tighten. "Yeah."

"Hi."

"How are you? I mean, how is your leg? Or well all of you?" She thumped herself on the forehead.

"It's okay, I guess. It's taking longer to heal than we thought it would."

"I wanted to make sure I hadn't missed your call, you know, all summer." She fluttered her eyelids.

"About that. I meant to call."

"Uh-huh."

"Really, I did."

"But somehow the whole summer whizzed by." She wanted him to confess his love, ask for her forgiveness, and tell her he'd be right over to see her, but she knew better.

"No, it wasn't that."

"You invited me to come visit and told me you'd call and you never did." Her moist hand made it difficult to hang on to the phone.

"But—"

"I deserved to be treated better than that."

"You're right."

She paused for a moment. "You were a . . . jerk."

"Guilty as charged." He admitted it so easily.

"Well, just so that's cleared up then." She closed her eyes.

"I'm sorry, Caitlyn."

"Yeah, me too. Take care of yourself, Travis."

She closed the phone. Somehow she didn't feel the way she had when she'd seen Justin in the bookstore. Perhaps it was because Travis still had a piece of her heart, something she'd have to find a way to rectify.

"I guess that's it. It wasn't as satisfying as I'd hoped."

"At least you told him what you thought."

Caitlyn nodded. "He and Alison can live happily ever after." Caitlyn took the paper she'd saved all summer and ripped it in pieces. She threw the pieces up in the air and said, "Travis really is history and I'm done thinking about him."

thirty-two

"Guess who I saw in the parking lot?" Brittany asked.

"The Queen of England?" Caitlyn placed a half-filled milk jug back in the refrigerator.

"Very funny. It was Chase. He asked about you."

Caitlyn smiled. She grabbed her glass of milk and took a sip.

"I thought you weren't interested in Chase," Brittany said.

"That was then. This is a new semester and I'm ready to move on with my life." Caitlyn drank the rest of her milk, normal milk that came from a jug, which came from a store, not from a cow.

Someone knocked at the door. Brittany answered it. "Come on in, Chase."

Caitlyn smoothed her hair and cleared her throat. "Hi."

"Hi, Caitlyn. Good to see you." He smiled.

"You, too." He looked good. His tan set off his blond hair and made him quite attractive.

"When did you get back?"

"Yesterday."

"I wanted to come over and say hi. I better get back."

Caitlyn stepped closer to Chase. "Do you want to get together sometime?"

Chase took a step back. "Really?"

Caitlyn nodded.

"That'd be great."

"See you around then."

Chase left, and she shut the door behind him.

"That's so not cool," Brittany said with her arms folded across her chest.

"What?" Caitlyn flounced her hair.

"Using poor Chase."

"I'm not using him. Besides, you really aren't one to lecture me about this."

"You're still mad at Travis."

"No," she paused, "I'm over Travis." Caitlyn walked past Brittany.

"I don't believe you."

Caitlyn turned around. "You don't have to."

Brittany shook her head. "Before Darren, I might have been a little noncommittal—"

"A little? You were drooling over every guy we saw."

"The point is Chase likes you. You don't like him, and you know it."

Caitlyn shrugged and walked into her bedroom. She shut the door and screamed silently to herself. Brit knew her too well. She wasn't over Travis. But Travis was over her, and it was time to move on. Maybe Chase would prove to be a good friend, maybe more. She wasn't going to waste her time like she did after Justin. Carrying on after Travis wasn't going to change anything.

Caitlyn heard her phone ring. "Brit, can you get my phone?"

No answer.

"Brit?"

Again, no response. Caitlyn opened her door and ran to answer the phone. "Hello?"

"Cait?"

"Hannah? Where are you?" Caitlyn sat on the couch.

"I'm at home."

"Why? School's about to start. When will you be here?"

"I'm not coming back."

"Why not?"

"I've decided to serve a mission." Hannah's voice was calm.

"Whoa, that's random."

"My experience with Dave made me think about my life. After a lot of prayer and visits with my bishop, I decided that serving a mission was the right thing to do."

"That's cool. We'll miss you, though."

"I'll miss you, too. But this is what I'm supposed to do." Hannah sounded more self-assured than Caitlyn ever remembered her sounding.

"Keep us updated."

"I will. You've been a good friend to me, Cait. Thanks again."

thirty-three

Caitlyn stood in the Wilkinson Center reading the most recent copy of the *Daily Universe*. Someone walked up behind her and leaned over her shoulder. He said, "Are you walking back to the apartments?"

Caitlyn spun around. "Chase, hi."

They walked through the Wilkinson Center and out onto the street. They cut across the parking lot of the law school and headed toward Ninth East.

"Thanks for walking with me. Brit was supposed to meet me, but ever since she and Darren got engaged, her mind has been somewhere else. I never thought I'd see Brit be engaged. It's weird."

"Would you like to go mini golfing tonight?

"Hmm. Mini golfing? How about a movie instead?"

"Sounds good." He stopped for a minute. "I tried to ask you out last spring, but you never gave me a chance."

"I'm sorry. Maybe we can make up for it now."

*   *   *

Caitlyn picked out a new pair of jeans and a bright yellow shirt that was fitted in the middle and accentuated her trim waist. She straightened her hair. The summer sun had lightened it a bit. Soon she had to decide, though, to either highlight it again or settle for the natural dirty blond color. Whatever the case, she was determined not to let Brittany touch her hair again. She sprayed some perfume on her wrist.

Brittany leaned in to the bathroom area. "Can't make a purse out of a sow's ear."

"What?"

"My grandma used to say that all the time when someone was trying to pretend to be someone they weren't."

Caitlyn rolled her eyes.

"You don't even like Chase."

"Will you stop?" Caitlyn gave her a look.

"Someone has to remind you."

"For your information, I've been getting to know him, and he's a nice guy. He's cute and he isn't dating anyone else—a big plus and good enough for me."

"Okay, but don't say I didn't tell you so. Darren and I are going out to dinner. We're going to set the date and plan the reception."

"Have fun. Glad it's you and not me." *Really.*

Brittany walked down the hall and into her bedroom. Caitlyn stared at herself in the mirror. "She doesn't know what she's talking about. Chase is a great guy and I like him. I do."

Chase picked her up, and they made small talk on the way to the theater. It was the same theater she'd attended with Travis on their date last spring. She pushed the thought from her mind because it didn't matter. Travis was then and Chase was now. She looked over at Chase and smiled at him.

After the previews were over, and the opening credits flashed across the screen, Chase placed his arm around her. She searched, but there wasn't any magic. She didn't feel the tingling sensation that surged through her when Travis did the same thing a few months before. She shook her head. Travis was then, and Chase was now. Maybe if she said it enough, she'd believe it.

*　　*　　*

"Thanks for the movie. I enjoyed it, even if it had more adventure than romance."

"Thank you for going." Chase leaned in and gave her a kiss. Nothing. No rapid heartbeat, no sweaty palms, no melting into his arms. Nothing.

"I better get in." Caitlyn gave him a wave and walked into the apartment. Maybe there weren't fireworks right now, but it could still happen.

*   *   *

"Darren and I were thinking about taking a drive up to Salt Lake and shopping at one of the malls. Do you and Chase want to come?" Brittany said.

"I thought the new engaged you didn't approve of me dating Chase," Caitlyn said with an air of sarcasm.

"Apparently, you're going to keep yanking him along so we might as well all get used to it. Maybe things will work out with him after all."

"Thanks for your support." Caitlyn shook her head.

"So, you'll go?"

"I can't. I already have a big assignment in biology and it's due on Tuesday," Caitlyn said.

"Come on, it'd be fun. You can work on your assignment later," Brittany said. "Unless, of course, you don't want to spend the day with Chase."

"That's not it. I like Chase."

Brittany gave her a look.

"I do."

"Call him, then."

"Fine. I will." Caitlyn pranced over to the couch, grabbed her phone, and called Chase.

*   *   *

Darren drove his old silver Honda Accord so Chase and Caitlyn sat in the back. They talked about the weather, skiing, and whether or not BYU's football team had what it would take to make a championship team.

At the mall, Chase took hold of Caitlyn's hand, and they did some window shopping.

"My sisters used to make me take them to the mall, and I'd end up staying for hours while they shopped," Chase said.

"So shopping isn't a favorite activity?"

"With you it's a lot more fun." He smiled and squeezed her hand.

"My sister, Lindsay, is the real shopper in my family. I like to look around a little but not spend my whole day at the mall. I'd rather go to the beach."

"Me, too. There's nothing better than surfing. I want to go back to San Diego after graduation and live there. I don't think I could settle too far away from the ocean."

"I love San Diego. We've gone there on vacation a few times. Sea World is so much fun."

Chase's eyes widened. "On our next break, we should go back to California together and visit each other's families."

"That'd be fun." Wouldn't it?

"Hey, guys, over here." Caitlyn looked over to see Brittany waving at them.

Caitlyn counted the bags in Brittany's hands and said, "You've had a successful day."

"Isn't shopping the best?" Brittany said. She reached over and hugged Darren from the side.

The drive back to Provo seemed especially long. Did they take the route by way of Nevada? Finally, they pulled into the parking lot.

"Thanks, Darren, for driving," Caitlyn said.

"You're welcome," Darren said.

Caitlyn opened her car door and let herself out. Chase followed her to the front door of her apartment. "Thanks for going, Chase."

"Maybe we can catch a movie on TV?"

"I don't think so. I have a big assignment I need to work on tonight."

"Okay. I'll see you at church tomorrow. Save me a seat." He leaned in and gave her a kiss.

Caitlyn leaned back, so Chase wouldn't get carried away. "See you tomorrow."

She opened the door and walked inside. She collapsed on the couch. After ten minutes or so, the door flew open and Brittany jumped inside.

"What a great day. Did you have fun with Chase? Looks like he's very interested in you."

Caitlyn gave a smile.

"You're not fooling me."

"What?"

"You can't force yourself to like Chase, hoping it'll take your mind off Travis."

"Don't you get tired?"

"Of what?"

"Beating this subject into the ground. You were the one that talked me into giving Travis a chance after Justin. I did. He blew me off. Now, I'm trying to get on with my life. Would you rather I crawl into a hole like I did after Justin?"

"No."

"Then why are you giving me such a hard time?"

"I'm sorry. I don't mean to. It's just that . . . ."

"What?"

"You and Travis had something. I mean," Brittany placed her hand across her chest, "I could even feel it."

Caitlyn shook her head. "Maybe we did, but now it's over."

"And you think Chase is the right one?"

"No."

"So why are you going out with him?"

Caitlyn gaped at her roommate. "Did you have a complete personality change while I was gone for the summer? You were the ultimate 'date 'em and drop 'em' poster girl."

"You're right." Brittany sat on the counter. "Of course, you're the one that made me realize that."

"Apparently, I've created a monster."

"I'm more aware of correct dating procedure now, that's all."

"Seriously? I don't see anything wrong with dating Chase. Maybe we'll fall in love. Eventually."

"Cait, admit it."

Caitlyn leaned her head back. "So he doesn't make me smile for no reason, or laugh, or make my heart beat so fast I think I'm having a heart attack, and I don't fantasize about marrying him. So what? That stuff is for the movies. Besides, we've only started dating. And after a few months, who knows where it could lead?"

"Admit it."

"What do you want from me?"

"Travis does all of those things for you."

Caitlyn covered her face with her hands and then dragged her fingers down her cheeks. "He did, remember, past tense. And you were the one that told me to date after Justin dropped me. I'm following your advice."

"That was different."

"How? Justin dumped me on our wedding day, and Travis dumped me before we could even get close to that. At least Travis saved me the bother of buying the dress, sending out the invitations, ordering the cake, and paying a deposit for the photographer."

"But you weren't actually in love with Justin."

"I'm not, repeat not, in love with Travis."

Brittany jumped off the counter and flopped on the couch beside Caitlyn. "What if Travis dropped into your life again?"

Caitlyn gave an exasperated breath.

"Well?"

"That's not going to happen. You were there when I called him. He's gone on with his life. He's probably engaged to what's-her-name."

"But what if he did?"

Caitlyn closed her eyes. She couldn't waste time fantasizing about something that would never happen. She had to live with reality and forget about Travis.

thirty-four

*L*ifting her heavy eyelids, Caitlyn barely recognized the display on her clock radio. Time to get up for church. She hit the snooze button and rolled over to her other side. Why did church have to start so early? Who even enjoyed getting up this early besides farmers and . . . well, it didn't matter who liked early mornings.

Ten minutes passed and the alarm sounded again. Caitlyn sat up in bed. She pulled her knees in to her chest. Chase would probably be looking for her at church. He was a decent guy and he deserved a chance, didn't he? So what if he didn't make her forget her name when he touched her hand. So what if he was safe. So what if he didn't make her laugh or challenge her wit. So what. He was here and that counted for something, didn't it?

"Are you getting up or what?" Brittany said through a crack in the door. "I don't want to be late. Darren will be waiting. Hurry."

Caitlyn mumbled to herself and threw the comforter off.

After Relief Society, Chase found her and stood close enough to share all of her personal space. "Hi, Caitlyn. Are you ready for Sunday school?"

"I think so."

They walked to the Sunday school room and sat toward the back. Chase told her a story about one of his roommates and she politely laughed at all the appropriate places.

Sacrament meeting was more of the same. Chase whispered a few comments to her, and she nodded.

After the meeting concluded, Chase said, "I thought we could eat lunch together at your apartment. I'll go back to my apartment to change clothes and be right over."

"I'm not sure what we have for lunch."

"No problem. I've got some leftover pizza and we can heat it up."

"Sounds yummy." Caitlyn was sure he'd recognize her facetious tone, but instead he smiled and scurried off to the parking lot.

"I was kidding," she said in a whisper, wondering if she was doing the right thing.

thirty-five

"Did Chase make the reservations for all of us?" Brittany sat on Caitlyn's bed and gazed into a hand mirror while she applied some mascara.

"He said he called the restaurant yesterday. Dinner at 7:00 on Friday," Caitlyn said.

"I'm so excited to go to Homecoming. I think the dance on the Heber Creeper under the moonlight will be so romantic."

Caitlyn nodded.

"I'm sorry I gave you such a hard time about Chase. You seem to be getting along."

"Yeah." Caitlyn half smiled.

"You've spent every weekend together and most weeknights, too."

"Do you finally approve of me and Chase?"

"Sure." Brittany shrugged. "He seems to treat you pretty good."

"He's been the first guy that hasn't broken my heart, and he's dependable. I know what to expect with Chase." Caitlyn pulled her hair into a ponytail.

"Isn't that a little boring?"

"No, actually, it's great. No hidden girlfriends. No leading me on. Works for me."

"No rapid heartbeat or unexplained excitement, either, right?" Caitlyn gave her a look.

"I know, I know." Brittany held her hands up. "I'm sorry. I'll quit. We can make the rest of our plans for Homecoming, okay?"

They were interrupted by a loud knock. "I'll get it," shouted Andra, one of their roommates.

Caitlyn's bedroom door opened wider and Andra entered. She handed Caitlyn a long box. "This is for you."

"Thanks," Caitlyn said and she shut the door.

Brittany pawed at the box. "Looks like Chase sent you flowers."

Caitlyn opened the box and pulled out a dozen red roses. She inhaled the soft scent deeply and said, "They're beautiful. He really is a nice guy."

"Maybe he's more spontaneous than we thought. Are you going to read the card?" Brittany reached into the box and handed a small white envelope to Caitlyn.

Caitlyn opened it, removed the card, and gasped. She covered her mouth while her heartbeat quadrupled. She felt as if the blood was draining from her face.

"Did he propose or something? That'd be spontaneous." Brittany grabbed the card and read it aloud. "Caitlyn, call me. Travis." Brittany practically screeched his name.

Caitlyn still covered her mouth with one hand while she clutched at her chest with the other. Tears formed in the corners of her eyes. Was she imagining the name on the card?

"Why does he want you to call him?"

Caitlyn closed her eyes and pursed her lips. Finally she said, "No idea."

"Maybe he feels bad about how he treated you, and he wants to apologize."

Caitlyn stared straight ahead.

"Are you going to call him?"

No response.

"Cait?"

Caitlyn still said nothing. She wasn't sure what to say or how to respond. This came out of nowhere, and the shock paralyzed her mind.

Brittany stood and paced. "You have to call."

"Why?"

"Aren't you curious why he sent you a dozen red roses?"

"No." Her lips said it, but her heart certainly didn't agree.

"Big, fat liar."

"He probably wants to tell me he's getting married or something." Caitlyn twisted her hair.

Brittany rolled her eyes. "Guys usually send roses to other girls when they're getting married. . . . Come on."

"But he was a jerk to me."

"Call him and see what he wants. Where's the number?"

"I ripped it up after the last phone call. Remember?"

Brittany spied Caitlyn's phone and snatched it. Before Caitlyn could stop her, she was scrolling through the numbers. "Well, what do you know, here's his phone number." Brittany held it up in front of Caitlyn.

"I thought I deleted it."

"Uh-huh." Brittany turned the phone over to face her and poised her other finger over the keypad.

"Don't you dare hit the send button."

Brittany smirked and said, "Either you call him or I will."

"Brit, don't do it."

"You know I will."

"Fine. Give me my phone, and I'll do it." Caitlyn hit the button. She recognized his voice as soon as he answered.

"Travis?"

"Yes?"

"This is Caitlyn."

"Hi, Caitlyn." She hoped he couldn't hear her thunderous heartbeat.

"I got the roses . . . thank you."

"You're welcome." His voice was gentle, like she remembered it.

"They're beautiful."

"I guess I'm a little late with a proper apology." He sounded shy.

"A little."

"I'd rather apologize in person."

Caitlyn raised her eyebrow. "That'd be difficult."

"Only if you're busy this weekend."

"Why? Are you going to be in Provo?" Her chest tightened and she struggled to breathe.

"No. But I've got a plane ticket in your name at the Salt Lake airport."

A plane ticket?

"I owe you a trip to Colorado."

Caitlyn cleared her throat. "This weekend?"

"Yes. Tomorrow."

"I don't know if I can do that." Her stomach twisted and she felt light-headed. A sudden surge of excitement pulsed through her limbs.

"The flight leaves Salt Lake tomorrow night at 7:45 on United."

"Can you hang on for a minute?" Caitlyn took the phone from her ear and placed her hand over it.

"What did he say?" Brittany whispered.

"He wants me to fly to his house tomorrow night."

Brittany's eyes grew large. "Serious?"

"What should I do?"

"Go. Don't think about it, just go."

"I don't know if this is a good idea."

"Tell him you'll be there." Brittany squeezed Caitlyn's arm.

Caitlyn raised the phone to her ear. "I guess I can make that flight."

"I'll pick you up at the airport."

"See you tomorrow, then."

"Caitlyn?"

"Yeah?"

"I'm looking forward to seeing you."

She hung up the phone and fell to the ground.

"Cait?" Brittany leaned over her.

Caitlyn stared at the ceiling. "I am in complete and total shock that he sent me roses and is flying me to his house. I have no idea why I said yes."

Brittany sang out, "Because you love him. You think he's gorgeous. You want to marry him."

Caitlyn held out her hand, and Brittany helped pull her to her feet. "I can't believe I'm going to Colorado tomorrow. Maybe, once I see him I can be over him. You know, like when I saw Justin, I finally knew it was over."

Brittany shook her head. "You are ridiculous."

"I don't know if I'm up to this." Caitlyn sighed.

"I only see one problem."

"Which is?" Caitlyn held her hands out.

"He's got blond hair and has been your constant companion since you came back to school."

"Oh, no. Chase." Caitlyn slapped herself on the cheek.

"Yes, Chase."

Caitlyn laid her head back. "I didn't even think about him."

"Apparently."

"What should I say? That I'm flying off to Colorado on a whim."

"Something like that."

"Why didn't you remind me while I was on the phone?"

"And come between you and Travis? No way."

"It's not like Chase and I are engaged or anything."

"Maybe not yet, but I heard from one of his roommates that he's been shopping at some jewelry stores."

"Really?" Caitlyn covered her mouth.

"Yep."

"Why does this have to be so complicated?"

thirty-six

Alison, with her phone pressed to her ear, unpacked her small suitcase while she waited for Tanya to answer her call.

"Hello?" said Tanya.

"Hi, best friend."

"Hey, Alison. How's it going?"

"I'm still mad at you, you know. I can't believe you gave up coming back to BYU so you could hang out with Evan." Alison placed a salmon-colored shirt on the bed and straightened it out. "You're not engaged already, are you?"

"Not yet, but soon, I hope. Keep your fingers crossed for me."

Alison sat on her bed. "I knew it the minute you saw him at church."

"He's wonderful, isn't he?"

"And you've been virtually no help with our plan."

"Plan?"

"Getting me and Travis together." Alison finger-combed her hair.

"Oh, yeah. I guess I've been busy with Evan. He's so spiritual. And hot."

"Can we get back to me and Travis? You're losing your focus."

"Sorry."

"I decided to really step it up." Alison pulled a small box out of her purse.

"How?"

"I'm actually not in Provo."

"Are you here?"

"Yes. And, I'm going to break the rules and ask Travis to marry me." She smiled and clutched the small box in her hand.

"What?"

"I'm tired of waiting for him to make up his mind. We date for a while, then things cool off, and then we start dating again. It's time to get serious, get on with our lives, and get married."

"I thought he told you he wanted to be friends and that's all."

"He doesn't know what he wants. He needs me to take the lead. So I'm planning to come kidnap him tomorrow morning and take him up to the mountains and propose." Goose bumps covered her body as she considered her idea.

"That's too weird, Alison. Shouldn't you wait for him to do that?"

"Are you on my side or not?" Alison placed her hand on her hip.

"I want you two to get together, but I'm not sure you should propose to him. After all, if it's meant to be, he'll do the proposing, don't you think?"

"I thought you'd like this idea. I thought you, of all people, would be supportive."

"Well—"

"I'm done waiting for him. This is the right thing to do. Besides, our kids will love this story. Is he home?"

"I only got home a few minutes ago, but he's not here. He's been acting a little strange, though."

"How so?"

"I don't know, kind of nervous or something."

"Must be that he's sensing my visit. We're so connected. This is so exciting, don't you think?" Alison drew a deep breath and closed her eyes while visions of Travis, as her groom, danced across her mind.

"I guess."

"We're going to be sisters after all, like we've always planned. Maybe we can even have a double wedding, wouldn't that be awesome? I've almost paid off my wedding dress."

"I'll tell Travis you called. With our schedules I haven't seen him much this past week. And we're having company this weekend. Probably my aunt. I think she'll be here tonight or tomorrow. My mom said something but—"

"I'm planning to come over bright and early tomorrow morning with a picnic lunch and everything. He loves my picnics. I've planned it all perfectly."

"Isn't it a little cold for a picnic, especially in the mountains?"

"I'm bringing some hot chocolate, but we'll have to snuggle up close to keep each other warm. Don't tell him I called, though, I want to surprise him."

Alison hung up her phone and sprawled out across her bed. She felt giddy at the idea of finally being engaged to her one true love. Her dream was so close, she could almost reach out and hold it in her hands. By this time tomorrow, her life would never be the same.

thirty-seven

$\mathcal{S}$he wasn't sure if it was the turbulence, the impending landing, or the fact that she'd left Provo without telling Chase anything that made her want to vomit, but Caitlyn held the small white bag to her mouth and took several deep breaths. Why was she flying to the middle of nowhere in Colorado for an impulsive, possibly disastrous, trip?

The plane finally came to a jittery stop. She walked along the tarmac to the doorway. Step after step her breathing increased. Could someone her age have a heart attack? She grasped her chest and felt the perspiration trickle down the back of her neck. Panic set in as she imagined all sorts of scenarios.

She passed through the doorway and immediately spotted him. Her body convulsed while her pulse rate shot so high, she was certain she'd fall over dead right in front of him.

"Caitlyn." He grinned the same grin that had etched itself in her memory.

"Hi, Travis." She hoped her voice wasn't as shaky as it felt.

He handed her a large stuffed cow. "I thought this would help prepare you for your visit."

"Thank you. I think." Her ears warmed and she willed herself not to hyper-ventilate. He looked even better than she remembered.

"How was your flight?"

"A little bumpy."

"I'm glad you're here." He stepped in close and gave her a hug.

She melted into his arms. Her heart was pounding so hard, she was sure he could feel it against his chest.

He pulled back and said, "It's good to see you. My family is looking forward to meeting you."

"Sounds good." She glanced at his leg. "Looks like you're getting around better than the last time I saw you."

"The walking cast makes it a little more convenient. I got it a few days ago. Why don't we get your stuff and head out to my car? I had to get a new one after the accident."

Again, Caitlyn was intrigued by his choice in vehicles. This time it was a red, four-door Pontiac Grand Am. A family car.

Inside the car, silence covered them like heavy snow. Travis finally said, "I live about an hour from the airport."

"That should give us some time to talk."

Travis started up the engine, and they left the small airport. They followed a two lane highway lined with pine trees. When the trees cleared, Caitlyn noticed how the moonlight illuminated tall, jagged mountain peaks blanketed in snow.

The moon-kissed scenery was breathtaking. But she wanted to know what happened. Night after night during the long summer at home, she wondered why he hadn't called. Since she'd been back in Provo, she'd tried to fill her mind with school and social activities, but questions still nagged at her. She was almost afraid to ask, but knew if she didn't, she'd never know, and what was the point of this trip if she didn't understand what happened? "So," she paused, "I never heard a word from you all summer . . . Why?"

Travis raised his eyebrows. "That's direct and to the point."

"I've learned that if you want to know something, ask."

Travis ran his fingers through his dark, wavy hair. He cleared his throat and said, "I got home from Provo and wasn't doing too well. The drive was hard on me. I was laid up on the couch for about three weeks."

"I'm sorry. I had no idea." She softened a bit, but she was still determined to have an explanation. "And the rest of the summer?"

"I wanted you to come visit, but I was in pain, and there were some complications with my leg. I had to go back to the hospital because of an infection that was killing all the good bacteria in my stomach. After they got it under control and let me go home, a nurse was assigned to come and check on me to make sure I was doing okay."

"Alison?" She said it as nonjudgmental as possible, although she almost choked on the name.

"What?" Travis sounded surprised.

"She's a nurse, isn't she?"

"Yes, but—"

"At the hospital last spring, she told me she planned to take good care of you when she got home. Lots of tender loving care or something like that." Finally, she could vocalize her thoughts.

Silence again.

"Lost your voice?" She wanted an answer about Alison.

"Alison did come by frequently." After a few minutes of silence he added, "And we dated a bit."

"While you were on the couch? That must've been interesting." She clenched her teeth and reached up to twirl her hair.

"No, after I was up and around."

"So, you didn't answer my get-well card, and you didn't call me all summer because you were involved with Alison? Does that sum it up?" She stared at Travis.

He nodded.

"And now?"

"Wow, you don't believe in giving a guy a break do you?"

"Nope. I've had almost five months to ponder this situation. It's time you fessed up and told me the truth."

Several minutes passed. "You're right. You deserve the truth. I dated her for a little while, but I couldn't get you out of my mind."

"I wasn't in your mind enough to call me."

"Now, wait. I admit that wasn't too cool, but I felt like I needed to give my relationship with Alison a chance and see where it went."

"Where did it go, exactly?" She picked at the cuticles around her fingernails while she waited for his answer.

"Nowhere. You kept getting in the way. No matter how hard I tried to concentrate on her, you'd pop into my head."

A smile peeked around the edges of Caitlyn's mouth.

"I finally decided that I needed to see you again because I'd never be able to date anyone else until I did."

Caitlyn's smile broke into a wide grin. She turned to gaze outside the passenger window so he couldn't see her expression.

"I'd like another chance."

"I'm not sure I can do that."

"Why not? Is there someone else?"

"You could say that." He didn't need to know that Chase had only been a failed distraction.

"I've never been to Colorado and I thought it'd be fun to have a free trip." She was enjoying giving him a little of what she'd felt since last June.

After several minutes, Caitlyn turned and looked directly at him. "Wondering what's going on?"

"Yes."

"That's exactly how I've felt for months."

"You're not going to make this easy, are you?"

She shook her head. "Nope. I've been dumped enough."

"I didn't dump you."

"Okay, you ignored me for an extended period of time. Is that better?"

"I can see this is going to be a challenge." He looked over at her. "But I'm up to it."

"We'll see."

He reached over and placed his hand on hers. His touch sent electric vibrations through her veins.

*   *   *

The long dirt driveway leading to his family's home was different than she had imagined. The lane was bumpy and dusty and from the moonlight she could see a white, two-story farmhouse with a wrap-around porch.

"The lights downstairs are on. I think my parents will be up to meet you, but you may have to wait to meet everyone else in the morning."

Caitlyn bit her bottom lip. It was one thing to see Travis again, but meeting his whole family was something else. At least she had the rest of the night before she had to meet them, especially since her past meeting in the hospital with Tanya hadn't been too smooth.

Travis pulled in front of the house and shut off the engine. Caitlyn could see a bunch of people standing on the front porch.

"Looks like everyone waited up to meet you after all." So much for meeting the rest of the family the next day.

He opened the door for her and grabbed her hand. They walked up to the porch.

"This is Caitlyn, everyone." He turned to her, "Caitlyn, this is everyone."

Her eyes grew large.

"Don't worry, I'll give you names to go with the faces."

Caitlyn gave a weak smile.

"You've met my mom."

"Hi," Caitlyn said.

His mom smiled the same warm smile she remembered from the hospital.

"This is my dad."

His father, with thinning dark hair and dark blue eyes like Travis's, reached out his hand and shook Caitlyn's. "Welcome to our home. It's nice to meet you."

"Thank you," Caitlyn said in a soft voice.

Travis continued, "The tall one with short hair is Shanna, and Julie is the one with blond hair and braces. Julie doesn't really fit into the family because we picked her up at a flea market for a real cheap price."

"Ha, ha, very funny," Julie said.

"Don't forget about me," said a small girl with long, dark braids.

"And this is Dawn. She's the baby of the family."

"I'm not a baby," Dawn said.

"I mean, the youngest." Travis flipped her braids.

"Are you gonna marry my brother?" Dawn asked through her toothless grin.

Caitlyn felt her face flush. Shanna stepped in front of Dawn and told her to be quiet.

"My brother, Greg, is still on his mission. And I don't see Tanya."

His mother said, "Tanya's out with Evan. She'll be back later."

"She's always out with Evan," Julie said.

Travis turned to Caitlyn, "Maybe you can see Tanya in the morning. You've already met her."

"Yes, I have," Caitlyn hoped it didn't come out too rudely.

"You've all met her, now go up to bed," his mother said.

"I hope you marry Travis—you're pretty," Dawn said as Shanna scooted her away.

Caitlyn smiled even though her cheeks were still on fire.

His mother said, "We're happy to have you and glad you had a safe trip, Caitlyn. Good night." She walked into the house.

"We'll see you in the morning," his dad said as he left.

Caitlyn noticed Dawn looking at her through the window and giggling. Caitlyn waved at her, and Dawn disappeared. "That was interesting."

"They like you."

"I'm not used to so many people in one house. My family is so much smaller. It must be quite an ordeal at dinner."

"Not really. I've had a large family all my life, so I guess I'm used to it. But we have several neighbors with eight, nine, and ten kids."

Caitlyn shook her head. "Wow."

"I love having kids around."

"A quiver full, right?"

Travis laughed. "Great memory."

Caitlyn crinkled her nose. "What's that smell?"

"What smell?"

"I can't really describe it, except that it smells disgusting." She glanced around.

"It's probably the dairy. We're upwind from them. Don't worry, you'll get used to it. Or it might be the pig pen. Sometimes it gets a little odiferous. I'm so used to it, though, I guess I can't smell it anymore. Should we go inside?"

"Sure."

"The bedroom you'll be staying in is upstairs."

Caitlyn followed him through the living room and up the stairs to the first room on the right. It was painted a light shade of lavender and decorated with ribbons and certificates with 4-H on them.

"Shanna's won Best of Breed for the last two years at the county fair."

"Huh?"

"Best of Breed for her ewes." He placed her small suitcase on the bed.

"Her what?" Caitlyn blinked her eyes several times.

"Female sheep."

"Oh."

"I earned a lot of my mission money from my 4-H steers and hogs. It's hard work."

Travis spoke a language she didn't understand, and she felt like she was in a foreign country.

"I hope you like the room. Shanna and Julie worked hard getting it ready. The bathroom is down the hall." He pointed to his left.

"Thanks."

"Maybe we should turn in. It's late and I've got a full day planned tomorrow."

"You do?"

Travis smiled.

Caitlyn reached up and twirled her hair. "I'll see you in the morning."

"You bet." He winked at her and closed the door.

She sat on the bed and let herself fall back. A million thoughts waltzed across her mind. She hardly knew this guy and his way of life was completely opposite from the one she knew. She was sure they'd never find a middle ground. Was it a mistake to come?

thirty-eight

Caitlyn heard a knock at her door. "Hello?"

"Are you awake?" Travis said.

She cleared her throat. "Yes."

"My mom will have breakfast ready in a few minutes."

"Okay." She jumped up from the bed. Although she'd been awake since the sun first peeked through the window, she hadn't gotten dressed or put on her makeup. She'd spent most of the night listening to strange animal noises and chirping insects while she tossed and turned, trying to figure things out.

When Travis disappeared from her life, she'd tried to unwrap him from her heart. But now that she was with him again, she realized how unsuccessful she'd been at loosening his grip. She sat on the edge of the bed.

She didn't want to get hurt again. She'd had enough misery. She wasn't ready to toss her apprehension out the window. She was going to play it cool and take her time.

After several minutes, a knock sounded at the door again. Caitlyn opened it and Travis stood in the doorway in a flannel shirt, faded blue jeans, and cowboy boots. He had his cowboy hat in his hands.

"Morning, miss, ready for some grub?" He grinned and tipped his head

"I think so."

"How'd you sleep?"

"Okay, except for the cricket concert and other weird noises."

Travis laughed. He reached out his hand and took Caitlyn by hers. Together they descended the stairs to the kitchen where the family was seated around a large wooden dining table.

"Good morning," his mom said.

"Smells wonderful," Caitlyn said.

His mom pointed to two chairs near the other end of the table. She said, "Tanya isn't down quite yet, but we'll say the blessing and she'll join us soon."

After the blessing was offered by Shanna, the chattering began, and plates of eggs, sausages, pancakes, and bacon rounded the table.

"How do you like it here so far, Caitlyn?" Julie said as she scooped some pancakes onto her plate.

"It's nice. Very different from where I grew up in California." Caitlyn took a few sausages and passed the plate to Shanna.

"Did you get to spend day after day at the beach? I bet you were super tan all the time." Shanna said.

"I did spend a lot of time at the beach, but I had to go to school and work, too."

"Can you surf?" Julie said.

Caitlyn laughed. "A little."

"Not everyone surfs in California, Julie," Travis said.

Caitlyn took a bite of her bacon. "This is delicious, Mrs. Dixon. Thank you."

"You're welcome, Caitlyn."

Travis smiled.

"What?" Caitlyn looked at him.

"George tastes pretty good, doesn't he?"

"George?"

"The bacon, he was . . ."

Caitlyn shook her head. "Please, don't tell me."

He let out a laugh.

"Travis, stop it," his mother said.

"It's okay, Mrs. Dixon, I think he enjoys the fact that I'm such a city girl."

Caitlyn sipped some fresh milk. It tasted a bit stronger and fuller than the store-bought milk she was used to.

"Tell us about your family, Caitlyn," his dad said.

A voice from the stairs carried into the kitchen. "Mmmm, I can smell bacon. Georgie's going to taste good this morning." Tanya rushed into the kitchen. As soon as she caught a glimpse of Caitlyn, she froze. She looked over at Travis with a strange expression.

"Tanya, you remember Caitlyn, right? You met her at the hospital," Travis said.

Tanya's gaze settled on Caitlyn. "Uh, yeah. What are you doing here . . . at our house?"

"Remember I told you we were having company this weekend," her mom said.

"I thought it was Aunt Lorna or someone like that."

"Maybe you didn't hear Mom because you've been so obsessed with Evan every day and night," Julie said. She and Shanna giggled.

Tanya gave her younger sisters a look. She suddenly covered her mouth.

"What's wrong?" Travis's mom stood.

"I need a phone. Does anyone know where a phone is?" Tanya's eyes were wide.

"Are you okay?" Travis's dad said.

"I need to call . . . Evan. That's it. I need to call Evan." Tanya gave a small smile.

A knock sounded at the door.

"I'll get it. It's probably Evan. I won't need to call him, I guess." She laughed nervously.

"Tanya, you're acting even weirder than usual," Julie said.

"And that's pretty weird," Shanna said.

"I'll get the door," Travis said.

"No, no, I'll get it." Tanya ran over to the door. She opened it and struggled to keep it partially closed. "Wait, let me talk to you,"

Tanya said as the door pushed open.

Alison stepped past Tanya. She had a picnic basket hanging off her arm and she sang out, "Oh, Trav. Surprise, surprise."

Julie gasped, Shanna laughed, and Caitlyn wanted to evaporate.

thirty-nine

"I can't believe that girl is here, in your house, and you didn't tell me. How could you let me come over here like this and she's sitting right there. Why is she here? Did she force herself over here to trap Travis? I should tell her what I think of her. Who does she think she is, coming here and trying to move in on Travis!" Alison paced back and forth in Tanya's bedroom.

"Calm down, you're getting all worked up," Tanya said. She rested her hand on Alison's shoulder, but Alison jerked away.

"It's because you've been so wrapped up in yourself and that Evan. You're so selfish. You've ruined everything."

"Me?" Tanya took a few steps back.

"You were supposed to be helping me. What happened to all of our plans?"

"I don't know."

"I do. You've become so absorbed in your own life you've completely forgotten about mine. You're supposed to be my best friend, and we're supposed to be sisters."

Tanya faced Alison. "Has it occurred to you that Travis has other ideas?"

"You mean that girl downstairs? Hmph. You can't be serious. He couldn't possibly be interested in her."

"So why is she here?"

"I don't know. But it's time to straighten it all out."

"I don't think—"

"And you shouldn't, Tanya, because it obviously doesn't suit you. I'll have to take care of this myself. Travis doesn't even know what's best for him. He thinks he does, but . . . I need to explain it to him and get rid of that girl once and for all. She's been nothing but a nuisance ever since his accident." Alison flipped her head back.

"She has a name, you know."

Alison felt as if her blood were boiling. "Who cares?"

"I think Travis does."

Alison glared at Tanya. "How dare you say that. I'm the one that's right for him and you know it."

Tanya sat on the bed. "I'm not so sure anymore."

"What?" Alison narrowed her eyes. "Are you going to betray our friendship after all of these years and give up our plan?"

"Maybe our plan didn't include one of the most important parts."

"Like what?"

"Travis's feelings. He should make up his own mind without interference."

Alison's heartbeat increased, and she was finding it difficult to control her rage. She raised her hands up in the air. "I can't believe what I'm hearing."

"You should talk to Travis yourself."

Alison shook her finger at Tanya. "You're on thin ice for being my best friend."

"Maybe you're not the friend I thought you were after all. Meeting Evan and being with him has made me realize what true love is. You can't plan it. You can't make it happen."

"Whatever." Alison shook her head, her fury about to explode. "And don't even tell me you think Travis is in love with that girl. He loves me."

"I don't know, Alison. He hasn't told me. But I'd guess he's very interested in her if she's here."

"She probably drove over here and surprised him. He probably didn't even expect her and now he's being nice so she doesn't feel bad for coming all the way out here. I'm sure that's it."

A knock sounded at the bedroom door.

"Yes?" Tanya said.

"Can I come in?" Travis said.

Tanya opened the door, and he walked in.

Alison swallowed her anger and put a smile on her face. "Hi, Trav. How are you?"

"I'm sorry, Alison," Travis said.

"About what?" she said it sweetly and as innocently as possible.

"I didn't know you were in town."

"It was a spur of the moment thing. I wanted to surprise you." She placed her hand on his arm.

Travis stepped away. "You surprised me all right."

Alison smiled. "I have a delicious picnic lunch ready for us. I even packed marshmallows for the hot chocolate."

"I can't do that."

"Because of Catherine."

"It's Caitlyn."

"Oh, yes. I can wait while you explain everything to her. I'm sure your mom and Tanya will keep her company." She looked directly into his eyes and then added, "I have something important to ask you."

Travis clasped his hands together. "Alison, I owe you an apology."

"For what?"

"I think you might have the wrong idea."

"I do?" She straightened. What was he talking about? How could she have the wrong idea?

"We're friends."

Alison sighed with relief. "I'm so glad to hear you say that." She glanced over at Tanya. "See, I told you. Just tell her to go home so you and I can spend the weekend together." She stepped close to Travis, inhaling his familiar cologne.

Travis held his hands up. "No, Alison. I mean, you and I are just friends."

"Excuse me?" She jerked her head back.

"I'm really sorry if I've given you the idea that there was something more than that."

"But we've been dating."

"We dated."

"So what was that?" Alison felt like her chest was collapsing.

"I told you when I helped you move back to Provo that I thought it was better if we didn't see each other anymore."

"You were tired from the trip. You didn't mean it." She attempted to smile, though tears welled up in her eyes.

"Yes, I did."

"You don't know what you're saying."

His voice was calm as he said, "I know exactly what I'm saying."

"But we should be together. We went to prom, wrote while you were on your mission, we've been dating. I don't understand. We're meant to be together." She emphasized her pleading with her hands because she had to make him understand.

"I love Caitlyn."

Alison's voice exploded, "What?"

"From the moment I met her, my life's been different."

"What about this past summer?"

Travis was silent for a moment. He let out a breath and said, "I thought you and I should see if there was anything between us, but I kept thinking about Caitlyn. It wasn't fair to you, and I'm sorry. I didn't mean to hurt you."

"I can't believe you think you love her. How could you?" She felt like someone was plunging a knife into her chest and twisting it.

He shrugged. "I just do. And I'm going to—"

Alison held her hand up. "Don't even say it. I don't want to hear it." She bit back her sadness.

"I'm sorry. Really."

Alison stiffened, rage overcoming her sorrow. Through

clenched teeth she said, "It's your loss. Believe me, you're the one that needs sympathy if you think she'll ever make you happy. I'm the right one for you, but if you're too blind to see that, then you don't deserve me."

forty

Caitlyn stood on the porch biting at her thumbnail and wondering what was happening between Travis and Alison. The last person she thought she'd see was Alison, which was fine by her. Alison had been so rude at the hospital and Caitlyn had tossed over in her mind what she'd say to her if she ever had the opportunity. Of course, part of her feared what Travis would think if she ever did tell Alison what she thought of her.

The front door flew open. Alison let out a scream as she stomped through the doorway. She whipped her head around and narrowed her eyes as she approached Caitlyn. "You."

Caitlyn stared back at her without flinching. Time to either let go of her fear and stand up to Alison or shrink back and always regret it.

"Who do you think you are coming out here?" Alison spat it out like venom.

Caitlyn contemplated how to reply. She didn't want to stoop to Alison's level or drive Travis away, but she didn't want to be ripped apart either. With a smile she said, "Travis invited me. Is that a problem?"

"You think you're so smart, don't you?"

Caitlyn's smile evolved into a grin.

Alison glared at Caitlyn, and Caitlyn almost expected to be turned into a frog.

"Take that smug look off your face before I knock it off."

With her heart beating wildly, she said, "I'd like to see you try."

Alison stepped back. "Like I'd even want to touch you."

Caitlyn raised her eyebrows and shrugged.

"You have no idea how to make him happy." Alison took a step toward Caitlyn, so Caitlyn backed up a few steps toward the front door.

With a confident smile Caitlyn said, "But I'm sure going to try. And by the look of things, there's not a thing you can do about it, Agnes."

"How dare you!" Alison lunged forward, and Caitlyn stepped back again, against the door. Alison moved in closer. Without warning, the front door opened and pushed Caitlyn forward causing her to stumble into Alison. Alison lost her footing and both Caitlyn and Alison tumbled down the steps. A struggle ensued and they rolled along the walkway. When they stopped, Caitlyn had Alison pinned to the ground.

"Get off me, you cow," Alison screeched. She pushed Caitlyn off her and sat up. Caitlyn attempted to stand but didn't notice Julie, who was carrying a bucket of fresh eggs. Caitlyn knocked into Julie and the bucket flew into the air.

As if viewing a slow motion movie, Caitlyn watched the bucket descend and scatter the eggs. A lone egg hit Alison on the head and splattered all over.

"Ooo," Alison screamed with yolk running down her forehead and dripping onto her cheek.

Travis rushed over to them. "Are you okay?"

"No! She did that on purpose!" Alison shrieked.

Caitlyn tried to protest, but got a case of the giggles instead. She turned to Travis and said, "I didn't mean to—"

"Oh, yes she did," Alison huffed. "Look at how she's treated me, Trav. How can you—"

"Maybe you should go home and wash up," Travis said, offering his hand to help Alison up.

"Don't touch me. I don't need anything from you." Alison stood and stomped off to her car.

"What happened?" Tanya asked as she rushed out the door.

"Alison's going home to wash the egg off her face," Travis said with a serious expression. He glanced over at Caitlyn, and they both started laughing.

*　　*　　*

"Let's take a walk. I want to show you some of our place," Travis said.

They walked in silence toward a grove of cottonwood trees. The air smelled wet and Caitlyn could hear the water as it rushed across the boulders. Fall had painted the scenery in different shades of brown while the bare trees waved their branches in the brisk breeze.

"I guess it's a little cold for a walk. Your nose is pink." Travis smiled.

Caitlyn held up her hands to her face.

"Your hands look a little cold, too. Let me warm them up." Travis took her hands in his.

For several moments they stood, locked in each other's gaze. Caitlyn momentarily forgot how to breathe.

They returned to the house and met Tanya on the porch.

"Caitlyn," Tanya said. "Could we talk?"

"Sure."

"Alone?" Tanya glanced at Travis.

He looked at Caitlyn and then walked into the house.

Tanya took a seat on one of the front steps and Caitlyn followed suit.

After a few minutes, Tanya said. "I owe you an apology. I wasn't very nice to you when I met you in the hospital."

Caitlyn nodded.

"Alison and I have been best friends forever. We used to plan out our weddings and everything. My dream groom changed but hers was always the same one."

Caitlyn could guess who played that part.

"She's always planned to marry Travis. I'm sure he's told you that they've dated on and off for a long time."

"He mentioned it."

"When we realized you were at the hospital so much and that Travis seemed interested, we got carried away. Alison was determined to get you out of the way, and I went along because she was my best friend."

Caitlyn didn't say anything.

"Today, though, I realized that she's out of control. Travis should choose who he wants to marry."

"I agree."

"I hope you can accept my apology and forgive me for the way I acted."

Caitlyn smiled. "You got it."

"Are you two done yet?" Travis said through a crack in the door.

"Yep." Tanya said. "You can have her back." Tanya stood and walked back into the house.

*　　*　　*

That evening Travis and Caitlyn drove along an unlit dirt road that wound around, back and forth, as it edged higher in the mountains. Snow appeared on the sides of the road. Travis stopped the car. "We can't go much farther or we'll hit too much snow. Let's get out for a minute."

He walked around the front of the car and opened Caitlyn's door. He led her back to his side of the car. He leaned in through the window and turned up the song playing on his CD. Caitlyn didn't recognize the song, but the melody was distinctively country. As she listened to the words about being amazed, the song seemed to express exactly how she felt.

Travis pulled her into him and began swaying to the music. He sang the words to the song softly in her ear and her legs felt like spaghetti. She never wanted the moment to end as they danced under the blanket of black sky adorned with shimmering stars.

As they danced next to his car, Caitlyn felt as if they were the only two people in the world. She never wanted the dance to end.

"I'm sorry," he said simply.

"What?"

"Everything with Alison."

Caitlyn pulled away and leaned against the car. "Maybe she's right."

"Huh?"

"The two of you have so much in common and you've known each other for so long, maybe—"

He pulled her so close to his chest, she could hardly breathe. Her face was only inches from his. He peered deeply into her eyes and said, "I know exactly what I want."

"And that is?"

"To marry you."

Caitlyn's cheeks throbbed while her breath caught in her throat.

"I love you, and I want to marry you."

Suddenly, memories of waiting for Justin on their wedding day rushed her with the ferocity of an unexpected wave. Fear insinuated itself in the caverns of her mind. She staggered to the front of the car.

Travis followed her. "Did I say something wrong?"

"This was a mistake. I shouldn't have—"

"Come here?"

Caitlyn nodded.

"Why did you come?"

Caitlyn struggled to keep her voice even. "I don't know. I've never seen Colorado—I thought it'd be fun."

He moved in close, his hot breath tickling her ear as he whispered, "That's all?" She trembled in his arms.

She summoned her strength and stepped away from him. "I'm not ready to—"

"Trust me?"

Caitlyn blinked her eyes.

"I know you were hurt before."

She tilted her head. "How do you know about Justin?"

"Justin?" He studied her. "I meant that I hurt you by not calling during the summer."

"Oh."

"Who's Justin?"

Caitlyn shook her head. "It doesn't matter."

"It does to me."

Caitlyn said nothing for a few minutes. "Justin and I were together in high school. He was my first boyfriend, and we were in love, or so I thought. He went on his mission, I waited, he came home, we got engaged, and he dumped me for another girl the day of our wedding. At the temple. End of story." She folded her arms across her chest.

"That was harsh."

"So, you see, you weren't the first. And since you did abandon me for several months, I'm not sure I want to—"

He reached out and pulled her into him again. All of her thoughts fell from her mind. He caressed her cheek and softly said, "I'm sorry."

"Apology accepted." They stood, arms wrapped around each other until Caitlyn pulled away.

"Don't try to analyze this. Go with what you feel. I'm not going anywhere this time," Travis said.

Her heart thudded as he leaned in and gently laid his warm lips across hers. He kissed her tenderly for several moments. He then gazed at her and said, "Tell me you don't feel it."

"I . . . I . . . I . . ."

He kissed her again.

forty-one

The drive to the airport gave Travis and Caitlyn another uninterrupted time to talk. "Did you think about last night?" Travis said.

"Yes."

"Tell me what you're thinking." He caressed her hand.

"I'm not sure."

"It probably seems like this came out of nowhere."

Caitlyn nodded.

"I've never stopped thinking about you, and last month I decided I wanted to marry you."

Caitlyn shook her head. "But you didn't let me in on that, so this has happened really fast for me. I didn't hear from you for months, and now, all of a sudden, you're talking marriage." She ran her fingers through her hair. "I need some time."

"Take whatever time you need. Sooner or later, you'll figure out that you want to marry me." He grinned.

"You're pretty confident."

He nodded. "I should be, I've prayed about it and gotten my answer."

"What?" Caitlyn was taken aback by his statement. He'd prayed about them getting married?

"You should pray about it, too."

*　　*　　*

At the airport, Travis took Caitlyn's hand. He fastened a bracelet around her left wrist. "This is to remember your visit here and to remind you of me."

"Thank you." She admired the gold s-shaped links.

He hugged her. "I'll see you at the end of the week."

"What?" She pulled back.

"I'm driving to Provo to see you."

"You are?"

"Is that a problem?"

Caitlyn scrambled to figure out what to say. "It's Homecoming."

"Great. We'll plan to go."

"But—"

"You already have a date."

"Sort of."

"What does that mean?"

"Yes, I have a date." An image of Chase flashed through her mind.

"Cancel it."

"I can't cancel it. There are plans."

"Then, I'll sit at your apartment and wait until you're done. You can even introduce me to him."

"That wouldn't be awkward at all." She rolled her eyes. Aggravation poked her like a sticker bush. Maybe she didn't actually want to go with Chase, but Travis didn't need to make things even more difficult. And he seemed to be enjoying it.

"I don't mind. I can find a movie on TV or read a book. I'll find something to do while I wait."

"It's not that simple."

"Why not?"

Caitlyn placed her hands on her cheeks. She considered whether or not to tell him about Chase and finally decided it was best to be completely honest. Besides, Travis would get it out of her anyway.

"I've been dating someone since I came back to school. You dropped out of my life for months and then suddenly dropped back in. Chase doesn't even know I left."

Travis smirked. "Chase? That guy from our FHE group last spring?"

Caitlyn nodded. "He's a nice guy."

"He's history."

"Is that so?"

He stepped close to her and gazed into her eyes. "Yeah, that's so."

She struggled to keep her mind clear. "I need some time."

"You have six days."

"But—"

"Plenty of time to let him down. I'll see you next weekend." He winked, and Caitlyn felt the fluttering in her stomach.

She turned and walked through the door to the tarmac with her stuffed cow under her arm. She found her seat in the small plane, sat down, and buckled her seat belt.

The take off was smooth, so she leaned her head back against the headrest. Her thoughts swirled around her mind. She couldn't deny her feelings for Travis, but she was still apprehensive about jumping into a relationship with him, especially considering his track record—and hers. If only her head and her heart could agree.

And then there was Chase. He was a nice guy who was active in the Church. He'd served a mission and had never done anything but care about her. He'd never trashed her heart or made her want to scream in frustration. But the spark wasn't there. She didn't feel that onslaught of emotion at his touch. Yet he was safe and she could trust him.

Travis? He'd been a permanent resident in her mind ever since she first met him. Like a magnet to steel, she felt the powerful, inherent attraction. He made her laugh. He was strong and committed to the Church. But he'd ditched her once before. She couldn't take another Justin episode in front of the temple again. She patted the stuffed cow.

One thing was for sure, she couldn't keep both of them. She

had to make a decision. Chase was clueless about the whole situation; he didn't even know he deserved a decision, but he did. It wasn't going to be easy.

She closed her eyes and was surprised to find herself in Salt Lake City much sooner than she expected.

The drive back to Provo seemed shorter than usual, as she vacillated between Chase and Travis. It wasn't that she was in love with Chase, at least not yet, but she had no reason to fear he'd hurt her as she did with Travis. And maybe in time she'd fall in love with him.

Of course, she had to admit that she'd been in love with Travis for months and that scared her. Even if Alison were no longer a threat, she couldn't completely trust Travis to not run out on her.

Before she knew it, she was in the parking lot of her apartment. She got out of her car and admired the bracelet still on her left wrist. She made her way to her apartment.

"Cait, you're back," Brittany said from the hallway as Caitlyn stepped into the apartment. She ran to the front door and hugged Caitlyn. "Sit down and tell me all about it." Brittany grabbed the stuffed cow and looked it over.

"I don't even know where to start."

"By the way, Chase was here last night asking about you."

Caitlyn closed her eyes and shook her head. "What did you tell him?"

"I said you weren't home, and I wasn't sure when you'd be home. I didn't actually lie." Brittany gave a fake smile.

"What am I going to do?"

"We can talk about Chase later. Tell me about Travis."

Caitlyn hesitated.

"Oh, come on," Brittany insisted as she pushed Caitlyn.

Caitlyn tried to squash the smile poking around her mouth, but she failed. "He told me he loved me and wants to marry me."

Brittany fell back against the couch. "Serious?"

Caitlyn nodded.

"That's crazy."

"Isn't it? I can't marry him."

Brittany popped up. "Why not?"

Caitlyn attempted to push words out, but nothing came.

"Waiting . . ." Brittany said.

"He deserts me with no word for how long? Oh, yeah, months. Now he comes rushing back into my life and expects me to fall into his arms with no hesitation."

"Doesn't sound too bad," Brittany said.

"I don't want to—"

"Get hurt?"

"Yes."

"You've been singing that song long enough. It's been almost a year since Justin. And Travis isn't Justin."

"But he—"

"Is sure what he wants now. You've been in love with Travis ever since you first met him. Seems like the answer is pretty obvious."

"What about Chase?"

"You don't love Chase."

"I might." Caitlyn shrugged.

"No, you don't."

Caitlyn pointed her finger at Brittany. "But I can trust Chase. He's never hurt me and in time, I may fall in love with him."

Brittany slapped herself on the forehead. "It's simple. You love Travis. Marry him."

"What if he dumps me again?" Caitlyn tugged at her hair.

"What if he doesn't?"

Caitlyn let out a long breath. "Against my better judgment, I let myself fall for him last spring, and all it brought me was heartache the whole summer. I don't want to do that again."

"So you stay with Chase, the safe one? You deny yourself the one you really love in favor of the one you think won't hurt you? What sense does that make?"

"It makes sense to me." Caitlyn laid her hand over her chest.

"Then you're crazy because it sounds lame to me." Brittany jumped off the couch and made her way over to the kitchen.

"You're looking at it from your own perspective because you're in love with Darren, and he's never hurt you."

Over the refrigerator door, Brittany said, "Maybe Darren hasn't hurt me like Travis did you, but that doesn't make your reasoning right."

"I know. It's all jumbled in my head." Caitlyn rested her head in her hands. Through her fingers she said, "I don't know what to do."

*   *   *

Caitlyn adjusted her pajama pants and walked out into the living room. She froze where she stood.

"Hi, Caitlyn. One of your roommates let me in. You're a hard one to track down," Chase said.

Caitlyn swallowed hard.

"I missed you Friday night. Where were you? I wanted to take you to dinner."

Caitlyn licked her lips. "I went on a quick trip. Out of town. Unexpected."

"Is everything okay?"

"Yes, fine, thanks." She tried to relax.

"How about a drive?" He stepped close to her and rested his hand on her shoulder.

Caitlyn's thoughts shot back to her drive with Travis. "I'm kind of tired from my trip. Can I take a rain check?"

"Sure, I guess." He removed his hand.

"I'm sorry." She meant it in more ways than one.

"Can we get together tomorrow, after church?" Chase looked at her with puppy-dog eyes.

"Okay."

"Maybe we could drive up to the Mt. Timpanogos Temple?"

"That's sounds nice."

"It's a date." He smiled.

Caitlyn shut the door behind him.

"Who was that?" Brittany called out from the bathroom.

"Chase."

Brittany rushed down the hall, giggling. "What did he say?"

"He wants to go to the temple grounds tomorrow after church."

"Uh-oh. Sounds like proposal time."

"No way." Her nerves sizzled and a sickening feeling settled on her.

"His roommate was telling Darren how nervous Chase has been acting and that he put down some money on a ring." Brittany laughed again.

"This isn't funny." Caitlyn's stomach was twisted into a square knot.

"I know. Poor Chase."

"Chase? What about me?" Caitlyn held her hands out.

"I guess you'll need to make a decision one way or the other. Immediately, if not sooner."

"Justin couldn't wait to get rid of me and now—"

"You have two guys that want to marry you. How often does that happen?" Brittany tapped her on the arm.

"I don't know, but why did it have to happen to me?"

Caitlyn's phone rang. Brittany rushed to answer it. "Hello? . . . It's Brittany. How are you? . . . Good . . . Yes, she's right here." She handed the phone to Caitlyn and trotted off.

"Hello?"

"Hi, Caitlyn." She smiled at the sound of his voice.

"Hi."

"I wanted to make sure you made it home safe. How was your flight?"

"Fine." She didn't remember much of it.

"Have you thought about what I said?"

"A little." Actually, a lot. In fact, it was the main thing that had occupied her mind since last night.

"Do you still have your date Friday night?"

"Possibly."

"Why?"

"You can't drop back into my life and expect me to change everything." She chewed off the end of her fingernail.

"Why not?"

Caitlyn sighed. "It doesn't work that way."

"Caitlyn?" She loved how he said her name.

"Yes?"

"Are you going to pray about it?"

"I don't know."

"Are you afraid?"

"No." She wasn't, was she?

"I love you and I want to marry you."

"You said that."

"And?"

"What?" She twisted her hair around her finger.

"You love me, too. I know you do. But I can wait. Take all the time you need. Until Friday, of course." He laughed. "Good night, Caitlyn."

She hung up the phone. Travis was exasperating. She felt like she was on the roller coaster at Space Mountain in Disneyland. Up, down, up, down.

"How was Travis?" Brittany kissed at the air.

"He's planning to come this weekend. And he wants me to pray about marrying him."

"Are you going to?"

"I don't know." She ran her fingers from both hands through her hair.

"You're afraid to, aren't you?"

Caitlyn didn't answer.

"You're afraid the answer is yes."

She placed her hands on her hips. "He thinks he can magically reappear in my life and get exactly what he wants."

"So, you want to make him work for it?"

"I don't want to let myself feel for him and then have him disappear again."

"He sounds like he's serious this time." Brittany leaned against the counter.

"Maybe."

"And Chase?"

"I don't want to hurt his feelings."

Brittany grabbed a pretzel from the counter and popped it in her mouth. "Would you marry him to not hurt his feelings?"

"No, of course not! That'd be a disaster."

"Isn't the choice clear?"

"This is giving me a headache. I'm going to bed."

"You'll have to make up your mind before tomorrow afternoon."

Caitlyn gave Brittany a look. "Can you give me a little more pressure?"

Caitlyn trudged back to her bedroom and shut the door behind her. She fell on her bed. When Travis held her in his arms, the rest of the world melted away.

But Chase was a great guy who'd never hurt her or made her feel sad. There was something to be said about that. He was a good person, and he'd make a good, trustworthy, dependable husband. Maybe the chemistry thing was too glamorized. Maybe Chase was her obvious choice.

The more she thought about it, the more her head ached and her eyes stung. This was the most important decision she'd ever make, and it couldn't be wrong. She weighed it out in her mind. Back and forth she thought of Chase and Travis. Was she willing to take a risk on Travis? Could she face her fears of possible abandonment?

Finally, she'd tossed it around her mind as much as she could. She made a decision. It was time to pray about it and receive her answer.

She poured her feelings out in prayer. When she vocalized her decision, her chest felt as if it were on fire, a definite witness that her decision was correct and acceptable to Heavenly Father. As soon as she concluded the prayer, the peaceful assurance rested on her like a favorite blanket. It was clear-cut and now it was time to let go of her fears, put faith in her answer, and act on it.

forty-two

Chase and Caitlyn pulled into the Mt. Timpanogos temple parking lot. "This is my favorite temple. Let's get out and take a walk," Chase said as he tapped his pants pocket.

Caitlyn's nerves sent waves of nausea through her stomach. "First, I have something to say."

He put his finger to her lips. "I don't want you to say anything." He opened his door and jumped out.

"But . . ." It hung in the air over the empty driver's seat.

Chase practically danced around the front of his old brown Chevy Citation and opened her door. He stuck out his hand, and she placed her hand in his. Not even a crackle of electricity.

"Chase, there's something I need to tell you." She planted her feet, building her courage to tell him about Travis.

"Shhh. Don't say anything." He pulled her toward the temple. They stopped at a place near a tree where they could still see Angel Moroni. "Caitlyn, there's something important I want to ask you."

Her mind worked feverishly trying to come up with something, anything, to stop him.

"I've thought about this all week and I know you're the one for me." He bent down on one knee and pulled a box from his pocket. "Will you marry me?"

"I . . ." She felt like the first time she tried to swim across the pool by herself—scared, afraid of drowning, and helpless.

"It's a little sudden, I know, but I love you, and I want you to be my wife. You make me feel so happy when we're together." His smile stretched across his face. "You don't have to answer right now." He opened the box. Inside was a small solitaire diamond on a simple gold band.

"It's beautiful."

"When you give me your answer, I'll place it on your finger. Maybe you'll wear it at Homecoming?"

"I don't know what to say." Which was true, she had no idea how to tell him Travis had already proposed to her.

"I promise to always love you, Caitlyn. I'll do my best to be the kind of husband you deserve."

He pulled her close to him. She didn't want to hurt him but couldn't find the right words, so she said nothing.

*   *   *

"Travis will be here tomorrow, right?" Brittany said. She slurped soup from a plastic bowl.

"Yeah. He's going to stay with one of his cousins for the weekend."

"Are you nervous?"

"That'd sum it up." Caitlyn bit off a piece of toast.

"And you're still sort of engaged to Chase, or at least he thinks so?"

"It's a mess, I know." Caitlyn spun the soup around in her bowl.

"You should've told Chase right away."

"I know," Caitlyn gazed at the ceiling, "but I couldn't. I've been able to avoid him for the last few days. If only I could do that forever."

"Do you want to marry Chase?" Brittany took a piece of toast and shoved it in her mouth.

Caitlyn whirled her soup in the opposite direction. "He's been so nice to me, and he's never hurt me, but no, I don't want to marry him. I need to find the right time to tell him." She stuck her finger in the middle of her toast.

"Before Travis gets here?" Brittany raised her eyebrows.

"Preferably."

A knock sounded.

"I'll get it," Caitlyn said.

She opened the door and let out a shriek. "Travis?"

"I decided to come a day early." He smiled and grabbed her into an embrace. She could smell his subtle cologne and feel his warm skin next to hers as she tried to quell her inner lightning storm.

"How about some dinner? I'm starving." He glanced around the apartment.

"I, um, well—"

Brittany interrupted, "Caitlyn and I have already eaten." She pointed to the table.

"Looks appetizing. Let's go out and get a real meal."

"We like soup and toast, it's one of our regulars. We're not much for cooking," Brittany said with a laugh. She glanced at the living room window. "Uh, Caitlyn can I see you for a minute? Back in the bathroom?" She yanked Caitlyn down the hall and pushed her into the bathroom.

"What?" Caitlyn said.

"I saw Chase through the window. I bet he's on his way over here."

"That could be bad." Caitlyn twisted her hair.

"No kidding. You better take care of this. This'd be funny if it wasn't going to be so awful."

Caitlyn placed her hands on her face then pulled them down. She bit her lip and twisted her hair tighter and tighter. "I didn't mean for this to happen. I had no idea Travis would come a day early and I haven't figured out how to let Chase down without hurting him."

"It's going to be a lot worse now." Brittany shook her head.

"Can we open the window in Andra's bedroom and I'll jump out?"

"That won't solve it."

"You're right. I have to stop being afraid and deal with the whole thing. It's now or never, I guess." Caitlyn stood up straight. She took a deep breath and stepped out into hall. She froze. She could hear Travis and Chase talking.

She summoned all of her strength and courage. She walked into the living room with as much conviction as possible. Travis and Chase both turned to face her.

Brittany walked up behind her. "Travis?"

"Yes?"

"I'm having a problem with my car. It's making this really weird sound. Do you think you could come out and take a look at it?"

"Sure. I'm not a great mechanic, unless it's farm equipment."

"That's okay, I'm sure you're better than I am." Brittany laughed.

Caitlyn gave her a grateful look as Brittany took Travis out the door.

"Seems like he's doing okay from his accident," Chase said.

Caitlyn gave a quick nod.

"Do you have an answer for me?" Chase moved in close to Caitlyn and caressed her shoulders.

Caitlyn backed away and said, "Let's sit down."

Chase sat on the edge of the couch. He smiled and gazed at Caitlyn.

A few awkward minutes passed while Caitlyn's stomach flip-flopped. Her palms began to sweat as she tried to think what to say. She knew how it felt to be dumped, and she didn't want Chase to feel that way. But, she couldn't agree to marry him, either. She stammered, "I . . . I . . .I . . ."

The door opened. "I couldn't find a thing wrong with her car. Are you ready for dinner, Caitlyn?" Travis said.

"Dinner?" Chase said with a bewildered tone. He stood. "What's going on?"

Caitlyn stood and glanced between Chase and Travis.

"I'm taking my future wife out for dinner." Travis answered with a grin.

"Your what?" Chase said. He looked directly at Caitlyn.

Caitlyn turned away, unable to handle the hurt in his eyes.

"She hasn't given me a definite answer yet, but I think after tonight she'll be my fiancée." Travis placed his arm around Caitlyn.

"Caitlyn?" Chase asked.

"Um . . ."

"Caitlyn?" Travis asked.

"Whoa, this is bad." Caitlyn bit her lip.

"I think we deserve an explanation." Chase tapped his foot on the ground.

"You're right, you do."

"So?" Travis said.

Caitlyn covered her face for a moment. She removed her hands and said, "Okay. Chase has asked me to marry him."

"He has?" Travis asked as he jerked his head back.

"And," she turned to Chase, "Travis has asked me to marry him."

"What?" Chase's voice rose an octave.

"Wow, I never thought I'd be in this situation." Caitlyn wiped at her face.

She turned to Chase, "You've been so nice to me. You've never hurt me. I enjoy being with you. I—"

"Yes?" Travis and Chase said it together.

Caitlyn's throat was as dry as the sidewalk. It was time to stop being afraid once and for all. This moment would determine the rest of her life, and eternity, and she had to have the courage and faith to do the right thing. "I love Travis."

"I see." Chase took a few steps back, a hardened look crossed his face.

"I'm so sorry, Chase. I tried to tell you at the temple grounds, but you wouldn't let me."

Chase seemed to want to say something, but he said nothing.

"I'm sorry," Caitlyn said with as much sincerity as possible.

Chase turned around and marched out the door. Caitlyn followed him and watched him rush from her apartment. She shut the door and leaned against it. Now she understood how Justin had made a similar choice and, though it had hurt her, she could finally understand it. Justin didn't love her, and she didn't love Chase.

She made her way to the couch and sat down in a heap. It wasn't that she wanted to marry Chase, but she felt bad that she'd hurt him, and she could empathize.

"How 'bout you and me taking a walk?" Travis reached out his hand.

They walked down the street in front of the apartments. Caitlyn searched for the right words, hoping she'd be able to explain the situation to Travis, and herself. Finally, she said, "You deserve an explanation."

"I'm listening."

"After you dumped me, I started dating Chase. I didn't think I'd ever see you again, especially after I called and told you off for how you treated me—"

"A bright spot for me, I know."

Caitlyn gave him a look. "As I was saying, Chase and I have been dating since school started, and he took it a little more seriously than I did. I honestly didn't think he wanted to get married. It happened so fast."

"And?"

"When he asked me to marry him, I didn't know what to say. I didn't want to hurt his feelings. But, since I'd spent the weekend with you . . . well . . ."

"Go on, this is the good part." He rubbed his hands together.

"I'm not saying anything else."

Travis stopped. He stepped in front of Caitlyn and peered into her eyes. "Tell me you don't want to marry me."

"I . . ."

He leaned in and gently kissed her. He stepped back and said, "Tell me we aren't meant to be together. You can't deny it, Caitlyn. I love you."

"I love you, too."

"Marry me."

"Okay."

"Okay?"

"Yes, Travis, I will marry you."

forty-three

Caitlyn gazed at herself in the mirror in her beaded, long sleeved, figure flattering bridal gown.

Her mom stepped around to face Caitlyn. She placed her hand under Caitlyn's chin and nudged it up a bit. "You seem a little sad for your wedding day."

"It's just that . . ."

"I know, honey, I wish your dad were here, too."

"I feel bad that he'll miss the ceremony and has to wait outside the temple."

"Someday, we'll all be in here together." Her mom caressed her on the shoulder.

"You really think so, Mom?"

"Yes, I do."

"Aren't you afraid?"

"No, I'm not. You can't have fear and faith at the same time."

"I think I finally know that."

"Deep down, your dad is proud of your decision, even if he can't admit it right now. Enough about that. This is your wedding day." Her mom smiled and a tear rolled down her cheek.

"And Travis is here in the temple, only a few feet away, waiting to marry me. He said he'd marry me, and he kept his word. He didn't ditch me. He really is the one."

"He loves you so deeply." Her mother looked at her in the mirror. "You'll be happy together."

"Once I stopped being afraid he'd leave me and put my faith in him, and in us, I've never been so completely happy." Caitlyn wiped at her eyes.

*   *   *

"Ready to face the world as Mr. and Mrs. Travis Dixon?" Travis said, dressed in a white tuxedo. He squeezed her hand.

She smiled and squeezed his hand back. "Absolutely."

The doors to the courtyard behind the Los Angeles temple opened and Caitlyn and Travis emerged. Caitlyn searched the crowd that thronged the patio area. She spotted her Dad and Lindsay. Travis met his family, and they all exchanged hugs.

Her father hugged her tightly.

"I love you, Dad."

"I love you, too, Caitie." She could feel her father's tears on her neck.

"My turn," Lindsay squealed. She grabbed Caitlyn and said, "I can't believe you're married. You are so totally beautiful."

"Thanks, Linds."

Lindsay whispered in her ear, "Don't worry about Dad. He'll be okay."

Caitlyn looked at her baby sister who'd suddenly grown into a woman and said, "I know. A little bit of faith can go a long way."

Caitlyn stepped back and was seized by her roommates.

"Brit, thanks for coming. I'm so happy to see you. Two more weeks and I can come to your sealing."

"After your honeymoon, of course." Brittany grinned.

"Of course." They giggled and embraced.

"I knew you and Travis would end up together. I told you he wasn't Justin."

"You were right about all of it, and I've never been so happy."

Caitlyn turned to Hannah and said, "I can't believe you came all this way for my wedding."

They hugged and Hannah said, "I'm so happy for you, Cait."

"Thanks. You have to let us know when you get your mission call."

"Should be pretty soon."

"Believe me, it's definitely worth the wait to go to the temple. It's worth any sacrifice." Caitlyn glanced over at her dad.

"Thank you for helping me make the right decision," Hannah said.

"You're welcome." They hugged again.

Tanya stepped forward with Travis close behind. "Welcome to the family. Travis made the right choice, and I'm glad you'll be my sister."

"I knew you'd get married," Dawn said with a huge smile that swallowed her face.

Travis grabbed Caitlyn. He whispered in her ear, "I will love you for all of eternity, Mrs. Dixon."

"I guess Bishop Greene was even more inspired than he thought when he called us to be the mom and dad of our FHE group," Caitlyn said.

"I can't wait to start our own, real family." Travis tickled her.

She laughed and then said, "A quiver full?"

"Of course." Travis grinned the same grin that first captured her heart.

She gazed into his royal blue eyes, but this time, she didn't forget her name. Caitlyn Dixon.

And then she knew.

Love can't be planned. It just is.

book club questions

1. How do you develop a strong testimony of temple marriage?

2. How do you know when you've met the "right one?"

3. Why is it important to serve with conviction in your calling even when you don't particularly like the calling?

4. Can you have faith and fear at the same time? How did Caitlyn learn to have faith and not fear?

5. Caitlyn was willing to sacrifice having her dad attend her temple wedding. What have you had to sacrifice for the gospel? What should we be willing to sacrifice?

about the author

Rebecca was born and raised in Santa Barbara, California. She spent countless hours swimming in the ocean, collecting shells, and building sand castles.

She graduated from BYU with a Bachelor of Arts degree in Communications. While attending BYU, she met and married her sweetheart, Del.

Rebecca now lives in Colorado on a small ranch with a spoiled horse, a dog, goats, and a llama named Tina. She and Del have been blessed with ten creative and multi-talented children.

She has had numerous stories published in children's magazines, including the Friend and is the author of Heaven Scent, an LDS novel published by Cedar Fort, Inc.

Besides writing, Rebecca also enjoys dating her husband, playing with her kids, knitting, and dancing to disco music while she cleans the house. She's consumed at least 4,892 pounds of chocolate and even more ice cream (which is why she needs to dance while she cleans house).